DARK LAUGHTER

DARK
LAUGHTER

Sherwood Anderson

NEW YORK   MCMXXV
BONI & LIVERIGHT

COPYRIGHT 1925 ᐔᐧ BY
BONI & LIVERIGHT, Inc.
PRINTED IN THE UNITED STATES

First printing, September, 1925
Second printing, September, 1925
Third printing, October, 1925
Fourth printing, October, 1925
Fifth printing, November, 1925
Sixth printing, November, 1925
Seventh printing, December, 1925
Eighth printing, May, 1926
Ninth printing, October, 1926

DEDICATED
TO
JANE W. PRALL

BOOK ONE

DARK LAUGHTER

CHAPTER ONE

BRUCE DUDLEY stood near a window that was covered with flecks of paint and through which could be faintly seen, first a pile of empty boxes, then a more or less littered factory yard running down to a steep bluff, and beyond the brown waters of the Ohio River. Time very soon now to push the windows up. Spring would be coming soon now. Near Bruce at the next window, stood Sponge Martin, a thin wiry little old man with a heavy black mustache. Sponge chewed tobacco and had a wife who got drunk with him sometimes on pay-days. Several times a year, on the evening of such a day, the two did not dine at home but went to a restaurant on the side of the hill in the business part of the city of Old Harbor and there had dinner in style.

After eating they got sandwiches and two quarts of Kentucky-made "moon" whisky and went off fishing in the river. This only happened in the spring, summer and fall and when the nights were fair and the fish biting.

They built a fire of driftwood and sat around, having put out catfish lines. There was a place up river about four miles where there had formerly been, during the river's flush days, a small sawmill and a wood-yard for supplying river packets with fuel and they went there. It was a long walk and neither Sponge nor his wife was very young but they were both tough wiry little people and they had the corn whisky to cheer them on the way. The whisky was not colored to look like the whisky of commerce but was clear like water and very raw and burning to the throat and its effect was quick and lasting.

Being out to make a night of it they gathered wood to start a fire as soon as they had got to their favorite fishing place. Then everything was all right. Sponge had told Bruce dozens of times that his wife didn't mind anything. "She's as tough as a fox terrier," he said. Two children had been born to the couple earlier in life and the oldest, a boy, had got his leg cut off hopping on a train. Sponge spent two hundred and eighty dollars on doctors but might as well have saved the money. The kid had died after six weeks of suffering.

When he spoke of the other child, a girl playfully called Bugs Martin, Sponge got a little upset and chewed tobacco more vigorously than usual. She had been a rip-terror right from the start. No doing anything with her. You couldn't keep her away from the boys. Sponge tried and his wife tried but what good did it do?

Once, on a pay-day night in the month of October, when Sponge and his wife were up river at their favorite fishing place, they got home at five o'clock the next morning, both still a little lit up, and what did Bruce Dudley think they had found going on? Mind you, Bugs was only fifteen then. Well, Sponge had gone into the house ahead of his wife and there, on the new rag carpet in the front hallway was that kid asleep and beside her was a young man also asleep.

What a nerve! The young man was a fellow who worked in Mouser's grocery. He didn't live in Old Harbor any more. Heaven knows what had become of him. When he woke up and saw Sponge standing there with his hand on the door-knob he jumped up quick and lit out, almost knocking Sponge over as he rushed through the door. Sponge kicked at him but missed. He was pretty well lit up.

Then Sponge went after Bugs. He shook her till her teeth fairly rattled but did Bruce think she hollered? Not she! Whatever you might think of Bugs she was a game little kid.

She was fifteen when Sponge beat her up that time. He whacked her good. Now she was in a house in Cincinnati, Sponge thought. Now and then she wrote a letter to her mother and in the letters she always lied. What she said was that she was working in a store but that was the bunk. Sponge knew it was a lie because he had got the dope about her from a man who used to live in Old Harbor but who had a job in Cincinnati now. One night he went out to a house and saw Bugs there raising hell with a crowd of rich young Cincinnati sports but she never saw him. He kept himself in the background and then later wrote Sponge about it. What he said was that Sponge ought to try to straighten Bugs out but what was the use making a fuss. She had been that way since she was a kid, hadn't she?

And when you came right down to it what did that fellow want to butt in for. What was he doing in such a place—so high and mighty afterwards? He had better keep his nose in his own back yard. Sponge hadn't even shown the letter to his old woman. What was the use of getting her all worked up? If she wanted to believe that bunk about Bugs having a good job in a store why not let her? If Bugs ever came home on a visit, which she was always writing her mother some day maybe she would, Sponge wouldn't ever let on to her himself.

Sponge's old woman was all right. When she and Sponge were out that way, after catfish, and they had both taken five or six good stiff drinks of "moon," she was like a kid. She made Sponge feel—Lordy!

They were lying on a pile of half-rotten old saw-dust near the fire, right where the old wood-yard had been. When the old woman was a little lit up and acted like a kid it made Sponge feel that way too. It was a cinch the old woman was a good sport. Since he had married her, when he was a young man about twenty-two, Sponge hadn't ever fooled around any other women at all—except maybe a few times when he was away from home and was a little soused.

CHAPTER TWO

IT was a fancy notion all right, the one that had got Bruce Dudley into the position he was now in—working in a factory in the town of Old Harbor, Indiana, where he had lived as a child and as a young lad and where he was now masquerading as a workman under an assumed name. The name amused him. A thought flashing across the mind and John Stockton had become Bruce Dudley. Why not? For the time being anyway he was letting himself be anything that it pleased his fancy to be. He had got the name in an Illinois town to which he had come from the far south—from the city of New Orleans to be exact. That was when he was on his way back to Old Harbor to which he had also come following a whim. The Illinois town was one where he was to change cars. He had just walked along the main street of the town and had seen two signs over two stores, "Bruce, Smart and Feeble — Hardware" and "Dudley Brothers — Grocery."

It was like being a criminal. Perhaps he was a kind of criminal, had suddenly become one. It might well be that a criminal was but a man like himself who had suddenly stepped a little out of the beaten path most all men travel. Criminals took other people's lives or took goods that did not belong to them and he had taken—what? Himself? It might very well be put that way.

"Slave, do you think your own life belongs to you? Hocus, Pocus, now you see it and now you don't. Why not Bruce Dudley?"

Going about the town of Old Harbor as John Stockton might lead to complications. It wasn't likely anyone there would remember the shy boy who had been John Stockton, would recognize him in the man of thirty-four, but a lot of people might remember the boy's father, the school-teacher, Edward Stockton. It might even be that the two looked alike. "Like father like son, eh?" The name Bruce Dudley had a kind of something in it. It suggested solidity and respectability and Bruce had got an hour's amusement, while waiting for the train up to Old Harbor by walking about the streets of an Illinois town and trying to think of other possible Bruce Dudleys of the world. "Captain Bruce Dudley of the American Army, Bruce Dudley, Minister of the First Presbyterian Church of Hartford, Connecticut. But why Hartford? Well, why not Hartford? He, John Stockton, had never been to Hartford, Connecticut. Why had the place come into his mind? It stood for something, didn't it? Very likely it was because Mark Twain lived there for a long time and there had been a kind of connection between Mark Twain and a Presbyterian or a Congregational or a Baptist minister of Hartford. Also there was a kind of connection between Mark Twain and the Mississippi and Ohio Rivers and John Stockton had been fooling along, up and down the Mississippi River for six months on that day when he got off the train at the Illinois town bound for Old Harbor. And wasn't Old Harbor on the Ohio River?

> T'witchelty, T'weedlety, T'wadelty, T'wum,
> Catch a nigger by the thumb.

"Big slow river crawling down out of a wide rich fat valley between mountains far away. Steamboats on the river. Mates swearing and hitting niggers over the heads with clubs. Niggers singing, niggers dancing, niggers toting loads on their heads, nigger women having babies—easy and free—half white a lot of the babies."

The man who had been John Stockton and who suddenly, by a whim, became Bruce Dudley, had been thinking a lot about Mark Twain during the six months before he took the new name. Being near the river and on the river had made him think. It wasn't strange after all that he chanced to think of Hartford, Connecticut, too. "He did get all crusted up, that boy," he whispered to himself that day when he went about the streets of the Illinois town bearing for the first time the name Bruce Dudley.

"A man like that, eh—who had seen what that man had, a man who could write and feel and think a thing like that Huckleberry Finn, going up there to Hartford and—

> T'witchelty, T'weedlety, T'wadelty, T'wum,
> Catch a nigger by the thumb, eh?

"Oh, Lord!

"What a lot of fun to think, feel, cut the grapes, put some of the grapes of life into the mouth, spit the seeds out.

"Mark Twain, learning to be a river pilot on the Mississippi in the early days in the valley. What things he must have seen, felt, heard, thought! When he wrote a real book he had to put all aside, all he had learned, felt, thought, as a man, had to go back into childhood. He did it bouncing well, now didn't he?

"But suppose he had really tried to put into books a lot of what he had heard, felt, thought, seen as a man on the river. What a howl raised! He never did that, did he? Once he wrote a thing. He called it "Conversations in the Court of Queen Elizabeth," and he and his friends used to pass it around and chuckle over it.

"Had he got right down into the valley, in his day, as a man, let's say, he might have given us many memorable things, eh? It must have been a rich place, rank with life, fairly rancid with life.

"Big slow deep river crawling down between the mud banks of an empire. Corn growing rank up north. Rich Illinois, Iowa, Missouri lands getting their hair cut of tall trees and then corn growing. Down further south, forests still, hills, niggers. The river getting slowly bigger and bigger. Towns along the river —tough towns.

"Then—away down—moss growing on the banks of the rivers and the land of cotton and sugar-cane. More niggers.

" 'If you ain't never been loved by a brown skin you ain't never been loved at all.'

"After years of that — what — Hartford, Connecticut! Those other things — 'The Innocents Abroad,' 'Roughing It'—stale jokes piled up, everyone applauding.

> T'witchelty, T'weedlety, T'wadelty, T'wum,
> Catch your nigger by the thumb—

"Make a slave of him, eh? Tame the lad."

．　　　．　　　．　　　．

Bruce didn't look much like a factory hand. It had taken more than two months to grow a short thick beard and to let his mustache grow and while it was growing his face itched all the time. Why had he wanted to grow it? When he left Chicago and his wife he had cut out to a place called La Salle in Illinois and had started down the Illinois River in an open boat. Later he lost the boat and spent nearly two months, while he was growing the beard, in getting down river to New Orleans. It was a little trick he had always wanted to do. Since he was a kid and had read Huckleberry Finn, he had kept some such notion in mind. Nearly every man who lived long in the Mississippi Valley had that notion tucked away in him somewhere. The great river, lonely and empty now, was, in some queer way, like a lost river. It had come to represent the lost youth of Middle America perhaps. Song, laughter, profanity, the smell of goods, dancing niggers—life everywhere! Great gaudy boats on a river, lumber rafts floating down, voices across the silent nights, song, an empire unloading its wealth on the face of the waters of a river! When the Civil War came on, the Middle West got up and fought like the Old Harry because it didn't want its river taken away. In its youth the Middle West had breathed with the breathing of a river.

"The factory men were pretty smart, weren't they? First thing they did when they got the chance was to choke off the river, take the romance out of commerce. They may not have intended anything of the sort, romance and commerce were just natural enemies. They made the river as dead as a door-nail with their railroads and it has been that way ever since."

Big river, silent now. Creeping slowly down past mud banks, miserable little towns, the river as powerful as ever, strange as ever, but silent now, forgotten, neglected. A few tugs with strings of barges. No more gaudy boats, profanity, song, gamblers, excitement, life.

When he was working his way down river, Bruce Dudley had thought that Mark Twain, when he went back to visit the river after the railroads had choked to death the river life, that Mark might have written an epic then. He might have written of song killed, of laughter killed, of men herded into a new age of speed, of factories, of swift, fast-running trains. Instead of which he filled the book mostly with statistics, wrote stale jokes. Oh, well! You can't always be offending someone, can you, brother scribblers?

CHAPTER THREE

WHEN he had got to Old Harbor, the place of his boyhood, Bruce did not spend much time thinking of epics. That wasn't his lay just then. He was after something, had been after it for a year. What it was he couldn't have said in so many words. He had left his wife in Chicago, where she had a job on the same newspaper he had worked on, and suddenly, with less than three hundred dollars to go on, had started off on an adventure. There was a reason, he thought, but he was willing enough to let reason lie, for the time being anyway. His growing the beard had not been because his wife would make any special effort to find him when he turned up missing. It had been a whim. It was such fun to think of himself as going thus, unknown, mysteriously through life. Had he told his wife what he was going to do there would have been no end of talk, arguments, the rights of women, the rights of men.

They had been that kind in their relations to each other—he and Bernice—had got started together that way and had kept it up. Bruce hadn't thought his wife to blame. "I helped start things wrong myself—acted as though she were something superior," he thought, grinning. He remembered things he had said to her concerning her superiority, her mind, her talent. They had expressed a kind of hope that something graceful and fine would flash up out of her. Perhaps, in the beginning he had talked that way because he wanted to worship. She had half seemed the great person he had called her because he seemed to himself so worthless. He had played the game that way, not thinking much about it and she had fallen for it, had liked it, had taken what he said with entire seriousness and then he did not like what she had become, what he had helped make her.

Had he and Bernice ever had children perhaps what he had done would have been an impossibility, but they had none. She hadn't wanted any. "Not by a man like you. You're too flighty," she had said.

And Bruce was flighty. He knew it. Having drifted into newspaper work he had kept on drifting for ten years. All the time he had wanted to do something—write perhaps—but every time he had tried his own words and ideas, put down, made him weary. Perhaps he had got too deep into the newspaper cliché, the jargon—jargon of words, ideas, moods. As he had gone along Bruce had put words down on paper less and less. There was a way to be a newspaper man, get by, without writing at all. You phoned your stuff in, let someone else write it up. There were plenty of the scribbling kind of fellows about—word-slingers.

Fellows making a mess at words, writing the newspaper jargon. Every year it got worse and worse.

Deep in him perhaps Bruce had always had buried away a kind of inner tenderness about words, ideas, moods. He had wanted to experiment, slowly, going carefully, handling words as you might precious stones, giving them a setting.

It was a thing you didn't talk about too much. Too many people going into such things in a flashy way, getting cheap acclaim—Bernice, his wife, for example.

And then the war, "bunk-shooting" worse than ever —the very Government going into "bunk-shooting" on the grand scale.

Lord, what a time! Bruce had managed to keep himself on local stuff—murders, the capture of boot-leggers, fires, labor rows, but all the time he had got more and more bored, tired of it all.

As for his wife Bernice—he hadn't seemed to her to be getting anywhere either. She had both despised and in an odd way feared him. She had called him "flighty." Had he but succeeded, after ten years, in building up within himself a contempt for life?

In the factory at Old Harbor, where he was now working, automobile wheels were made and he had got a job in the varnishing room. He had been compelled to do something, being broke. There was a long room in a great brick building near the river-bank and the window that looked out into the factory yard. A boy brought the wheels in a truck and dumped them down beside a peg on which he put them one by one to lay on the varnish.

It had been lucky for him he had got the place beside Sponge Martin. He thought of him often enough in relation to the men with whom he had been associated ever since he had grown to manhood, intellectual men, newspaper reporters who wanted to write novels, women feminists, illustrators who drew pictures for the newspapers and for advertisements but who liked to have what they called a studio and to sit about talking of art and life.

Next to Sponge Martin, on the other side, was a surly fellow who hardly spoke all day long. Often Sponge winked and whispered to Bruce about him. "I'll tell you what's wrong. He thinks his wife is fooling around with another man here in town and she is, too, but he doesn't dare inquire into the matter too closely. He might find out that what he suspects is a fact so he just glums around," Sponge said.

As for Sponge himself, he had been a carriage-painter in the town of Old Harbor before anyone ever thought of building any such thing as a wheel factory there, before anyone had ever thought of any such thing as an automobile. On some days he talked altogether of the earlier days when he had owned his own shop. There was a kind of pride in him when he got on that subject and for his present job, varnishing wheels, only contempt. "Anyone could do it," he said. "Look at you. You ain't got no special hand for it but if you would pep up you could turn out almost as many wheels as I can and do 'em just as well."

But what was a fellow to do? Sponge could have been foreman of the factory finishing room if he had wanted to lick boots a little. One had to smile and kowtow a little when young Mr. Grey came around, which he only did about once a month.

The trouble with Sponge was that he had known

the Greys too long. Maybe young Grey had got it into his head that he, Sponge, was too much of a booze-hoister. He had known the Greys when this young one, that was now such a big bug, was just a kid. Once he had finished a carriage for old Grey. He used to come around to Sponge Martin's shop bringing his kid with him.

The carriage he was having built was sure a darby. It had been built by old Sil Mooney, who had a carriage-building shop right near Sponge Martin's finishing shop.

The description of the carriage built for Grey, the banker of Old Harbor, when Bruce was himself a boy and when Sponge had his own shop, took a whole after-noon. The old workman was so deft and quick with his brush that he could finish a wheel, catching every corner, without looking at it. Most of the men in the room worked in silence, but Sponge never stopped talk-ing. In the room at Bruce Dudley's back, behind a brick wall, there was a constant low rumble of machines but Sponge had got a trick of making his voice ride just above the racket. He pitched it in a certain key and every word came distinct and clear to the ears of his fellow workman.

Bruce watched Sponge's hands, tried to imitate the movement of his hands. The brush was held just so. There was a quick, soft movement. Sponge could fill his brush very full and yet handle it in such a way that the varnish did not drip down and he left no ugly thick places on the wheels he did. The stroke of the brush was like a caress.

[23]

Sponge talked of the days when he had a shop of his own and told the story of the carriage built for old Grey the banker. As he talked Bruce got a notion. He kept thinking of his having left his wife so lightly. There had been a sort of wordless quarrel—one of the sort they had often got into. Bernice did special articles for the Sunday paper and she had written a story that had been accepted by a magazine. Then she joined a writers' club in Chicago. All this had been going on and Bruce had not tried to do anything special on his own job. He had done just what he had to do, nothing more, and gradually Bernice had come to respect him less and less. It was evident she had a career before her. Writing special articles for Sunday newspapers, becoming a successful writer of magazine ,stories, eh? For a long time Bruce had gone along with her, going with her to meetings of the writers' club, going to studios where men and women sat talking. There was a place in Chicago, out near Forty-seventh Street near the park, where a lot of writers and painters lived, some low small building that had been put there during the World's Fair and Bernice had wanted him to go out there to live. She had wanted to associate more and more with people who wrote, made pictures, read books, talked of books and pictures. Now and then she spoke to Bruce in a certain way. Had she begun to patronize him a little?

He smiled at the thought of it, smiled at the thought of himself, now working in the factory beside Sponge Martin. One day he had gone with Bernice to a meat market—they were getting chops for dinner and he had noted the way an old fat meat-cutter in the place handled his tools. The sight had fascinated him and as he had stood in the place beside his wife, waiting her turn to be served, she began talking to him and he did not hear. What he was thinking about was the old meat-cutter, the deft quick hands of the old meat-cutter. They represented something to him. What was it? The man's hands had handled a quarter of beef with a sure quiet touch that represented to Bruce perhaps a way in which he would like to handle words. Well now, it might be that he did not want to handle words at all. He was a little afraid of words. They were such tricky, elusive things. It might be that he did not know what he wanted to handle. That might be what was the matter with him. Why not go and find out?

With his wife Bruce had come out of the place and had walked along a street, she still talking. Of what was she talking? Suddenly Bruce had realized he did not know,—did not care. When they got to their apartment she went to cook the chops and he sat by a window, looking into a city street. The building stood near a corner where men coming out from the downtown district got off north- and south-bound cars to take other cars going east or west and the evening rush hour had begun. Bruce worked on an evening paper and so would be free until early morning, but as soon as he and Bernice had consumed the chops she would go into a back room of the apartment and begin to write. Lord, what a lot of stuff she wrote! When she was not at work on her Sunday special stuff she worked on a story. She was at work on one just at that moment. It concerned a very lonely man in the city who while walking one evening saw in a shop window the wax dummy of what in the darkness he took to be a very beautiful woman. Something had happened to the street light at the corner where the shop stood and the man had for the moment thought the woman in the window alive. He had stood looking at her and she had looked back at him. It had been an exciting experience.

And then, you see, later, the man in Bernice's story had found out his absurd mistake, but he was as lonely as ever and kept going back to the shop window night after night. Sometimes the dummy woman was there and sometimes she had been taken away. She appeared now in one gown—now in another. She was in rich furs and was walking along a winter street. Now she had been arrayed in a summer frock and was standing on the shore of a sea or she was in a bathing costume and was about to plunge off into the sea.

The whole thing was a whimsical notion and Bernice had been excited about it. How would she make it turn out? One night after the street lamp at the corner had been fixed the light was so strong that the man could not help seeing that the woman he had come to love was made of wax. How would it be to have him take a cobblestone and break the street lamp? Then he might press his lips against the cold window-glass and run off down a side street never to be seen again.

T'wichelty, T'weedlety, T'wadelty, T'wum.

Bruce's wife Bernice would be a great writer some day, eh? Was he, Bruce, jealous of her? When they went together to one of the places where other newspaper men, illustrators, poets and young musicians gathered the people were inclined to look at Bernice, address their remarks to her rather than to him. She had a way of doing things for people. A young girl got out of college and wanted to be a journalist, or a young musician wanted to meet some man of power in the musical field and Bernice managed things for them. Gradually she had come to have a following in Chicago and was already planning to move on to New York. A New York paper had made her an offer and she was considering it. "You can get a job there as well as here," she had said to her husband.

As he stood beside his bench in the factory at Old Harbor, varnishing an automobile wheel, Bruce listened to the words of Sponge Martin, boasting of the days when he had a shop of his own and was finishing the carriage that had been built for the elder Grey. He described the wood that had been used, told how straight and fine the grain was, how every part had been carefully fitted into other parts. In the afternoon old Grey sometimes came to the shop after the bank was closed for the day and sometimes he brought his son with him. He was in a hurry for the job to be finished. Well, there was to be some kind of a special affair in the town on a certain day. The Governor of the State was to come and the banker was to entertain him. He wanted the new carriage to haul him up from the railroad station.

Sponge talked and talked, enjoying his own words, and Bruce listened, hearing every word while he kept right on having his own thoughts, too. How many times had he heard Sponge's story and how delightful it was to keep on hearing it. The moment had been the big one in Sponge Martin's life. The carriage couldn't be finished in the way it should be and be ready for the Governor's coming. That was all to it. In those days, when a man had his own shop, a man like old Grey might rave and rave, but what good did it do him? Silas Mooney, when he had built the carriage, had done a good job and did old Grey think that Sponge was going to turn round and do a bum, hurried job? They had it out one day, old Grey's kid, young Fred Grey, who now owned the wheel factory where Sponge worked as a common laborer, standing and listening. What Sponge thought was that young Grey got an earful that day. No doubt he thought, just because he owned a bank and because people like governors of states came to visit at his house, that his dad was a kind of God Almighty, but if he did he got his eyes opened that time anyway.

Old Grey got mad and began to swear. "It's my carriage and if I tell you to put on a few less coats and not to let each coat set so long before you rub it down and put on another you got to do what I say," he had declared, shaking his fist at Sponge.

Aha! And hadn't that been a moment for Sponge? Did Bruce want to know what he told old Grey? It had just happened that he had about four good shots in him that day and when he was a little lit up the Lord Almighty couldn't tell him how to do no job. He had walked up close to old Grey and had doubled up his fist. "Look here," he had said, "you're not so young any more and you're a little fat. You want to keep in mind you been sitting up there in that bank of yours too much. Suppose now you get gay with me and because you want that carriage in a hurry you come down here and try to take the job away from me or something like that. Do you know what will happen to you? You'll get kicked out, that's what will happen. I'll cave your fat face in with my fist, that's what will happen and if you get foxy and send anyone else down here I'll come up to your bank and maul you there, that's what I'll do."

Sponge had told the banker that. He wasn't going to be hurried into doing no bum job, not by him or anyone else. He had told the banker that and then when the banker had walked out of his shop, saying nothing, he had gone over to a corner saloon and had got a bottle of good whisky. Just to show old Grey something he had locked up his shop and knocked off for the day. "Let him haul his Governor in a livery hack." That's what he had said to himself. He had got the bottle of whisky and he and his old woman had gone fishing together. It had been one of the best parties they had ever been on. He had told the old woman about it and she had been tickled to death at what he had done. "You done just right," she had said. Then she had told Sponge that he was worth a dozen such men as old Grey. That might have been exaggerating a little but Sponge had liked to hear it all right. Bruce ought to have seen his old woman in them days. She was young then and as good-looking a skirt as there was in the state.

CHAPTER FOUR

WORDS flitting across the mind of Bruce Dudley, varnishing wheels in the factory of the Grey Wheel Company of Old Harbor, Indiana. Thoughts flitting across his mind. Drifting images. He had begun to get a little skill with his fingers. Could one in time get a little skill with thoughts, too? Could thoughts and images be laid on paper some day as Sponge Martin laid on varnish, never too thick, never too thin, never lumpy?

Sponge the workman telling old Grey to go to hell, offering to kick him out of his shop. The governor of a state riding in a livery hack because a workman wouldn't be hurried into doing a bum job. Bernice, his wife, at her typewriter in Chicago, doing special articles for the Sunday papers, writing that story about the man and the dummy wax figure of a woman in a shop window. Sponge Martin and his woman going off to celebrate because Sponge had told the local prince, the banker, to go to hell. The picture of a man and woman on a sawdust pile with a bottle beside them. A bonfire down near the river's edge. Catfish lines out. Bruce thought of the scene as taking place on a soft summer night. There were wonderful soft summer nights in the valley of the Ohio. Up and down river, above and below the hill on which Old Harbor stood, the land was low and in the winter the floods came up and covered the land. The floods left a soft silt on the land and it was rich, rank with richness. Wherever the land was not cultivated, weeds, flowers and tall flowering berry bushes grew thick.

They would be lying there on the sawdust pile, Sponge Martin and his wife, a little lit up, the fire blazing between them and the river, the catfish lines out, the air filled with smells, the soft fishy river smell, smells of blossoms, smells of things growing. It might be there would be a moon hanging over them.

The words Bruce had heard Sponge say—

"When she is a little lit up she acts like a kid and makes me feel like a kid too."

Lovers lying on an old sawdust pile under a summer moon on the banks of the Ohio.

BOOK TWO

CHAPTER FIVE

THAT story Bernice was writing about the man who saw the wax figure in a shop window and thought it was a woman.

Did Bruce really wonder how it had come out, what sort of an ending she had given it? To tell the truth he did not. There was something malicious in his thoughts of the story. It seemed to him absurd and childish and he was glad that it was so. Had Bernice really succeeded in the thing she had undertaken—so casually, in such an offhand way—the whole problem of their relation would have been somewhat different. "I would have had to look to my self-respect then," he thought. That grin would not have come so easily.

Sometimes Bernice used to talk—she and her friends talked a good deal. They all, the young illustrators and the writers who gathered in the rooms in the evenings to talk—well, they all worked in newspaper offices or in advertising offices just as Bruce did. They pretended to despise what they were doing but kept on doing it just the same. "We have to eat," they said. What a lot of talk there had been about the necessity of eating.

In Bruce Dudley's mind, as he listened to Sponge Martin's story of the defiance of the banker, was the memory of that evening when he had cut out from the apartment where he had lived with Bernice and from Chicago. He had been sitting by the front window of the apartment and looking out, and at the back of the apartment Bernice was cooking the chops. She would have potatoes and a salad. It would take her twenty minutes to cook the things and put them on the table. Then the two would sit down at the table to eat. How many evenings sitting down together like that—within two or three feet of each other physically and yet miles apart. They hadn't any children because Bernice had never wanted them. "I've got my work to do," she had said on the two or three occasions when he had spoken of the matter as they lay in bed together. She had said that but what she had meant was something else. She hadn't wanted to tie herself down, not to him, not to the man she had married. When she spoke of him to others she always laughed good-naturedly. "He's all right but he's flighty and he won't work. He isn't very ambitious," she sometimes said. Bernice and her friends had a way of speaking openly of their loves. They compared notes. Perhaps they used every little emotion they had as material for stories.

In the street before the window at which Bruce sat waiting for the chops and the potatoes a lot of men and women getting off street cars and waiting for other cars. Gray figures in a gray street. "If a man and a woman are so and so together—well, then they are so and so."

In the shop at Old Harbor, as when he had been a newspaper man in Chicago, the same thing always going on. Bruce had a technique of going along, doing the thing before him well enough while his mind went wool-gathering over the past and the present. Time ceased for him. In the shop, working beside Sponge, he had been thinking of Bernice, his wife, and now suddenly he began thinking of his father. What had happened to him? He had been a country school-teacher near Old Harbor in Indiana and then he had married another school-teacher who had come down there from Indianapolis. Then he had got a job in the town schools, and when Bruce was a small boy had got a place working on a newspaper in Indianapolis. The little family had moved there and the mother had died. Bruce went then to live with his grandmother and his father went to Chicago. He was there still. Now he worked in an advertising agency and had got himself another wife and with her three children. In the city Bruce had seen him, perhaps twice a month, when father and son lunched together at some down-town restaurant. His father had married a young wife and she didn't like Bernice and Bernice didn't like her. They got on each other's nerves.

Now Bruce was thinking old thoughts. His thoughts went around in a circle. Was that because he had wanted to be a man handling words, ideas, moods— and hadn't made it? The thoughts he had as he worked in the factory at Old Harbor had been in his mind before. They had been in his mind on a certain evening as the chops sizzled in the pan in the kitchen at the back of the apartment in which he had lived for a long time with Bernice. It was not his apartment.

When she had fixed it up Bernice had kept herself and her own wants in mind and that was as it should be. She wrote her Sunday special stuff there and also worked on her stories. Bruce did not need a place to write as he did little or no writing. "I only need a place to sleep," he had said to Bernice.

"The lonely man who fell in love with the dummy figure in the shop window, eh? Wonder how she will make it turn out. Why not have a sweet young girl, working in the store, step into the window some night? That would be the beginning of a romance. No, she will have to handle it in a more modern way. That would be too obvious."

Bruce's father was a funny chap. What a lot of enthusiasms he had gone through in his long life and now, although he was old and gray, when Bruce lunched with him he almost always had a new one. When the father and son went to lunch together they avoided speaking of their wives. Bruce suspected that because he had married a second wife who was almost as young as the son, his father always felt a little guilty in his presence. They never spoke of their wives. When they met in some Loop restaurant Bruce said, "Well, Dad, how's the kids?" Then the father spoke of his latest enthusiasm. He was an advertising writer and was sent out to write advertisements of soap, safety razors, automobiles. "I've got a new steam car account," he said. "The car is a whizz. It will run thirty miles on a gallon of kerosene oil. No gears to shift. As smooth and soft as riding in a boat on a calm sea. Lord, what power! They have to work out a few things yet but they'll do it all right. The man who invented this car is a wonder. The greatest mechanical genius I've ever seen yet. I'll tell you what, son, when this thing breaks it will smash the market for gasoline. You wait and see."

Bruce shifting nervously about in his chair in the restaurant as his father talked—Bruce unable to say anything when he went out with his wife among the Chicago intellectual and artistic set. There was Mrs. Douglas, the rich woman who had a country home and one in town and who wrote poetry and plays. Her husband owned a lot of property and was a connoisseur of the arts. Then there was the crowd over on Bruce's own paper. When the paper was down in the afternoon they sat about talking of Huysmans, Joyce, Ezra Pound and Lawrence. There was great pride in word-slinging. Such and such a man knew how to sling words. Little groups all over town talking of word men, sound men, color men and Bruce's wife, Bernice, knew them all. What was it all about, this eternal fussing about painting, music, writing? There was something in it. People couldn't let the subject alone. A man might write something, just knocking the props out from under all the artists Bruce had ever heard about—it wouldn't be hard he thought—but after the job was done it wouldn't prove anything either.

From where he had been sitting by the window of his apartment that evening in Chicago he could see men and women getting on and off street cars at the street intersection where the cross-town cars met the cars in and out of the Loop. God, what a world of people in

Chicago! At his own job he had to do a lot of running about through Chicago streets. He phoned most of his stuff in and some fellow in the office dressed it up. There was a young Jew in the office who could fairly make the words dance over the page. He did a lot of Bruce's stuff. What they liked about Bruce in the local room was that he was supposed to have a head. He had got a certain kind of reputation. His own wife didn't think he was much of a newspaper man and the young Jew thought he wasn't worth anything, but he got a lot of important assignments that the others wanted. He had a kind of knack. What he did was to get at the heart of the matter—something of that sort. Bruce smiled at the praise he was giving himself in his own thoughts. "I guess we've all got to keep telling ourselves we're some good or we would all go and jump in the river," he thought.

What a lot of people getting off one car and onto another. They had all been downtown working and now they were going to apartments much like the one in which he lived with his wife. What was his father like in his relations with his wife, the young wife he had got after Bruce's mother had died. With her he had got three children, ready-made, while by Bruce's mother he had never got but the one—Bruce himself. There had been plenty of time for more. Bruce was ten when his mother died. The grandmother with whom he had lived in Indianapolis was still alive. When she died she would no doubt leave Bruce her little fortune. She must be worth at least fifteen thousand. He hadn't written to her for over three months.

The men and women in the streets, such men and women as were now getting off and on the cars in the street before the apartment. Why did they all look so tired? What was the matter with them? What he had in his mind at the moment was not physical tiredness. In Chicago and in other cities he had visited the people were all inclined to have that tired, bored look on their faces when you caught them off guard, when they were walking along through the streets or standing at a street corner waiting for a car and Bruce had a fear that he looked the same way. Sometimes at night when he went off by himself, when Bernice was going to some party he wanted to avoid, he saw people eating in some café or sitting together in the park who didn't look bored. Downtown, in the Loop, during the day, people went along thinking of getting across the next street crossing. The crossing policeman was about to blow his whistle. They ran, little herds of them, like flocks of quails, escaping with their lives most of them. When they had got to the sidewalk on the other side a look of triumph.

Tom Wills, the man on the city desk down at the office, had a liking for Bruce. After the paper was down in the afternoon he and Bruce often went to a little German place where they could get drinks and had a pint of whisky between them. The German made Tom Wills a special rate on pretty good bootleg stuff because Tom steered a lot of people in there.

In a little back room they sat, Tom and Bruce, and

when they had taken a few pulls out of the bottle
Tom talked. He always said the same things. First
he cursed the war and condemned America for getting
into it and then cursed himself. "I'm no good," he
said. Tom was like all of the newspaper men Bruce
had ever known. He really wanted to write a novel
or a play and liked to talk about the matter to Bruce
because he didn't think Bruce had any such ambitions.
"You're a hard-boiled guy, ain't you?" he said.

He told Bruce of his plan. "There's a note I'd like
to strike. It's about impotence. Have you noticed,
going along the streets, that all of the people you see
are tired out, impotent?" he asked. "What is a newspaper—the most impotent thing in the world. What is
the theater? Have you gone much lately? They give
you such a weariness that your back aches, and the
movies, God, the movies are ten times worse, and if
this war isn't a sign of universal impotence, sweeping
over the world like a disease, then I don't know much.
A fellow I know, Hargrave of the *Eagle,* was out
there to that place called Hollywood. He was telling
me about it. He says all the people out there are like
fish with their fins cut off. They wriggle around trying
to make effective movements and can't do it. He says
they all have an inferiority complex something awful—
tired-out magazine writers gone out there to get rich
in their old age, all that sort of thing. The women all
trying to be ladies. Well, not trying to be ladies exactly. That isn't the idea. They are trying to look
like ladies and gentlemen, live in the kind of houses
ladies and gentlemen are supposed to live in, walk and

talk like ladies and gentlemen. It's such a God-awful mess, he says, as you never dreamed of and you got to bear in mind the movie people are America's pets. After you been there for a while, out in Los Angeles, Hargrave says, if you don't go jump in the sea you'll go crazy. He says the whole Pacific Coast is a lot like that—in that tone I mean—impotence crying out to God that it is beautiful, that it is big, that it is effective. Look at Chicago, too, 'I will,' that's our motto as a city. Did you know that? They got one out in San Francisco, too, Hargrave says, 'San Francisco knows how.' Knows how what? How to get the tired fish out there from Iowa, Illinois and Indiana, eh? Hargrave says that in Los Angeles the people walk along the street by the thousands with no place to go. A lot of smart guys, he says, sell them lots—places out on the desert—because they are too tired out to know their own minds. They buy and then go back into town and walk up and down the streets. He says a dog smelling a street post out there will make ten thousand people stop and look as though it was the most exciting event in the world. I suppose he exaggerates a little.

"And, anyway, I'm not bragging. When it comes to impotence if you can beat me you're a darby. What do I do? I sit at a desk and give out little slips. And what do you do? You take the slips, read them and run around town getting little items to be played up in the paper and you're so impotent you don't even write your own stuff. What's it all about? One day they murder someone in this town and get six lines out of it and on the next day if they do the same murder

[43]

they get played up all over every paper in town. It all depends what we got on just then. You know how it is. And I ought to be writing my novel, or a play, if I'm ever going to do it. If I write one about the only thing I know anything about, do you think anyone in the world would read it? Only thing I could possibly write about would be just about this stuff I'm always giving you—about impotence, what a lot of it there is. Do you think anyone wants that kind of stuff?"

CHAPTER SIX

ON that evening in the Chicago apartment Bruce sat having these thoughts and smiling softly to himself. For some reason Tom Wills, swearing at the impotence of American life, had always amused him. He, himself, did not think Tom was impotent. He thought the proof of the man's potence could have been found just in the fact that he got so mad when he talked. It took something in a man to be mad about anything. He had to have some juice in him to do that.

He had got up from the window to walk across the long studio room to where his wife Bernice had set the table, still wearing the smile, and it was just the kind of a smile that disconcerted Bernice. When he wore it he never talked because he was living outside himself and the people immediately about. They did not exist. For the time being nothing very real had any existence. Odd that at such times, when nothing in the world was very definite, he was himself the most likely to do some definite thing. At such a moment he could have lighted a fuse connected with a building filled with dynamite and could have blown up himself, all of the city of Chicago, all America, as calmly as he could have lighted a cigarette. Perhaps he was himself, at such times, a building filled with dynamite.

When he was that way Bernice was afraid of him and was ashamed of being afraid. Being afraid of anything made her seem less important to herself. Sometimes she grew sullenly silent and sometimes she tried to laugh it off. At such times she said Bruce had the air of an old Chinaman poking around in an alleyway.

The place in which Bruce then lived with his wife was one of the sort of places that are being fixed up nowadays in American cities to house just such childless couples as himself and Bernice. "Married couples who have no children and do not intend having any—people whose aspirations are above that," Tom Wills in one of his angry moods would have said. There were a lot of such places in New York City and in Chicago and they were fast coming into vogue in smaller cities like Detroit, Cleveland and Des Moines. They were called studio apartments.

The one Bernice had found and had fixed up for herself and Bruce had a long room at the front with a fireplace, a piano, a couch on which Bruce slept at night—when he did not go to Bernice, which he didn't very often—and back of that was a bedroom and a tiny kitchen. Bernice slept in the bedroom and wrote in the studio, and the bathroom was stuck in between the studio and Bernice's bedroom. When the couple ate at home they brought in something, usually from a delicatessen store, for the occasion, and Bernice served it on a folding table that could afterwards be put away in a closet. In what was called Bernice's bedroom there was a chest of drawers where Bruce kept his shirts and underwear, and his clothes had to be hung up in

Bernice's closet. "You should see me diving about the joint in the morning in my shift," he had once said to Tom Wills. "It's a shame Bernice isn't an illustrator. She might get some good stuff on modern city life from me in my B.V.D.'s. 'The lady novelist's husband getting all set for the day.' Some of that stuff the fellows put in the Sunday papers and call 'among us mortals.' 'Life as it is'—something of that sort. I don't look at the Sundays once a month, but you know what I mean. Why should I look at the things? I don't look at anything in any paper except my own stuff and I only do that to see what that smart Jew has managed to get out of it. If I had his brain I'd write something myself."

Bruce had walked slowly across the room toward the table where Bernice had already seated herself. On the wall back of her was a portrait of herself done by a young man who had been in Germany for a year or two after the Armistice and had come back filled with enthusiasm about the reawakening of German art. He had done Bernice in broad lines of color and had twisted her mouth a little to one side. One ear had been made twice the size of the other. That was for distortion's sake. Distortion often got effects you couldn't get at all by straight painting. The young man had been at a party in Bernice's apartment one evening when Bruce was there and had talked a lot, and a few days later, one afternoon when Bruce came from the office there the fellow was, sitting with Bernice. Bruce had had a feeling of having butted in where he wasn't wanted and had been embarrassed. It had been an awkward moment and Bruce had wanted to back out after putting his head in at the studio door, but had not known how to do it without embarrassing them. He had been compelled to do some fast thinking. "You'll excuse me," he said, "I have to go right out again. I've got an assignment on which I may have to work all night." He had said that and then had gone hurriedly through the studio and into Bernice's bedroom to change his shirt. He had felt it was up to him to change something. Was there something on between Bernice and the young chap? He hadn't cared much.

Afterwards he wondered about the portrait. He had wanted to ask Bernice about it but hadn't dared. What he had wanted to ask was why she had stood for it to be made to look as the portrait had made her look.

"It's for the sake of art, I guess," he thought, still smiling on the evening when he sat down with Bernice to the chops. Thoughts of Tom Wills talking, thoughts of the look on Bernice's face and on the young painter's face—that time he came suddenly in on them, thoughts of himself and the absurdities of his own mind and his own life. How could he help smiling although he knew the smile always upset Bernice? How could he explain that the smile had no more to do with her absurdities than with his own?

"For the sake of art," he thought, putting one of the chops on a plate and handing it to Bernice. His mind liked to play with phrases like that, silently and maliciously taunting her and himself too. Now she was sore at him because of the smile and the meal would be eaten in silence. After the meal he would go to sit by the window and Bernice would hurry out of the apartment to spend the evening with some of her friends. She couldn't very well order him out and he would sit tight—smiling.

Perhaps she would go back into her bedroom and work on that story. How would she make it come out? Suppose a policeman to come along and seeing the man enamored of the wax woman in the store window and thinking him crazy or a thief planning to break into the store—suppose the policeman should arrest the man. Bruce kept on smiling at his own thoughts. He imagined a conversation between the policeman and the young man, the young man trying to explain his loneliness and his love. In a bookstore downtown there was a young man Bruce had once seen at an artists' party to which he had once gone with Bernice and who had now, for some unexplainable reason to Bruce, become the hero of the tale Bernice was writing. The man in the bookstore was short, pale and wan and had a small neat black mustache and she had made her hero like that. Also he had extraordinarily thick lips and shining black eyes and Bruce remembered to have heard that he wrote poetry. It might be that he actually had fallen in love with a dummy figure in a store window and had told Bernice about it. Bruce thought that might be what a poet was like. Surely only a poet could fall in love with a dummy figure in a shop window.

"For the sake of art." The phrase kept running through his head like a refrain. He kept smiling and now Bernice was furious. He had at any rate succeeded in spoiling her dinner and her evening. That at any rate he had not intended. The poet and the wax woman would be left, hanging in air as it were, unfulfilled.

Bernice got up and stood over him, staring down at him across the small table. How furious she was! Was she going to strike him? What a strange puzzled baffled look in her eyes. Bruce looked up at her impersonally—as he might have looked out a window at a scene in the street. She did not say anything. Had it got beyond speech between them? If it had surely he was to blame. Would she dare strike him? Well, he knew she would not. Why did he keep smiling? That was what made her so furious. Better to go softly through life—let people alone. Did he have any special desire to torture Bernice and if he did, why? Now she wanted to have it out with him, to bite, strike, kick, like a furious little female animal, but it was a handicap Bernice had that when she was thoroughly worked up she could not talk. She just got a little white and that look came into her eyes. Bruce had an idea. Did she, his wife Bernice, hate and fear all men and was she making the hero of her story such a silly fellow because she wanted to make all men sing small? That would certainly make her, the female, loom larger. It might be that was what the whole feminist movement was about. Bernice had already written several stories and in all of them the men were like that chap in the book-shop. It was a little odd. Now she, herself, looked something like the chap in the book-shop.

"For the sake of art, eh?"

Bernice went hurriedly out of the room. Had she stayed, there was at least a chance he might have got her, as it was possible men sometimes got their women. "You come off your perch and I'll come off mine. Loosen up. Function as a woman and let me function as a man, with you." Was Bruce ready to have that happen? He thought he had always been ready for that—with Bernice or some other woman. When it came to the test why did Bernice always run away? Would she go into her bedroom and cry? Well, no. Bernice wasn't after all one of the crying sort. She would get out of the house until he had gone and then —when she was alone—would perhaps work on that story—the soft little poet and the wax woman in the window, eh? Bruce was perfectly aware of how malicious were his own thoughts. Once in a long time he had a notion Bernice wanted him to beat her. Could that be possible? If so, why? If a woman got that way in her relations with a man what brought it about?

Bruce having got himself into deep water by his own thoughts went to sit again by the window looking into the street. Both he and Bernice had left their chops uneaten. Whatever happened now Bernice would not come back into the room to sit while he was there, not on that evening, and the cold chops would lie like that, on the table over there. The couple had no servant. Every morning a woman came in for two hours to clean the place up. That was the way such establishments were run. Well, if she wanted to go out of the apartment it would be necessary for her to pass through the studio before his eyes. To slip out at the back door,

through an alleyway, would be beneath her dignity as
a woman. It would be a come-down for the female
sex—represented by Bernice—and she would never
lose her sense of the necessity of dignity—in the sex.

"For the sake of art." Why did that phrase stick
in Bruce's mind? It was a silly little refrain. Had
he been smiling all evening, making Bernice furious
by the smile—because of that phrase? What was art
anyway? Did such men as himself and Tom Wills
want to laugh at it? Did they incline to think of art
as a silly, mawkish sort of exhibitionism on the part
of silly people because to do so made them seem to
themselves rather grand and noble—above all such nonsense—something of that sort? Once when she was
not angry, when she was soberly in earnest, a short
time after their marriage, Bernice had said something
of that sort. That was before Bruce had succeeded in
breaking down something in her, her own self-respect,
perhaps. Did all men want to break something down
in women—make slaves of them? Bernice said they
did and for a long time he had believed her. Then
they had seemed to get on all right. Now things had
surely gone to pot.

After all it was evident that, as far as Tom Wills
was concerned, he, at bottom, cared more about art
than all the other people Bruce had known, certainly
more than Bernice or any of her friends. Bruce did
not think he knew or understood Bernice or her friends
very well but did think he knew Tom Wills. The man
was a perfectionist. To him art was something out
beyond reality, a fragrance touching the reality of

things through the fingers of a humble man filled
with love—something like that—a little perhaps like a
beautiful mistress to whom the man, the boy within the
man, wanted to bring all of the rich, beautiful things of
his mind, of his fancy. What he had to bring had
seemed to Tom Wills such a meager offering that the
thought of trying to make the offering made him
ashamed.

Although Bruce sat by the window pretending to look
out he was not seeing people in the street outside. Was
he waiting for Bernice to pass through the room, wanting to punish her a little more? "Am I becoming a
Sadist?" he asked himself. He sat with hands folded,
smiling, smoked a cigarette and looked at the floor and
the last feeling he was ever to have of the presence of
his wife Bernice was when she passed through the
room without his looking up.

And so she had made up her mind that she could
pass through the room, snubbing him. It had begun at
the meat market where he had been interested in the
hands of that meat-cutter cutting meat rather than in
what she was saying to him. What had she been talking about, her latest story or an idea for a special article
for the Sunday paper? Not having heard what she
said he could not remember. At any rate his mind
had checked her all right.

He heard her footsteps crossing the room where he
sat looking at the floor, but he was at that moment
thinking, not of her but of Tom Wills. He was doing
again what had made her angry in the first place, what
always made her angry when it happened. Perhaps he

was at just that moment smiling the peculiarly exasperating smile that always drove her half mad. What a fate that she should have to remember him thus. She would always be thinking that he was laughing at her —at her aspirations as a writer, at her pretensions to strength of will. There was no doubt she did make some such pretensions but then who didn't make pretensions of one kind or another?

Well, he and Bernice had sure got into a jam. She had dressed for the evening and went out saying nothing. Now she would spend the evening with her own friends, perhaps with that chap who worked in the bookstore or with the young painter who had been to Germany and had painted her portrait.

Bruce got up out of his chair and snapping on an electric light went to stand looking at the portrait. The distortion idea meant something to the European artists who began it no doubt, but he doubted the young man's knowing quite what it meant. How superior he was! Did he mean to set himself up—to decide offhand that he knew what the young man did not know?

He stood thus, looking at the portrait, and then suddenly his fingers, hanging at his side, felt something greasy and unpleasant. It was the cold uneaten chop on his own plate. His fingers touched it, felt it and then with a shrug of his shoulders he took a handkerchief out of his hip pocket and wiped his fingers. "T'witchelty, T'weedlety, T'wadelty, T'wum. Catch a nigger by the thumb." Suppose it were true that art was the most exacting thing in the world? It was true as a general thing that a certain type of men, who did not look physically very strong, almost always went in for the arts. When a fellow like himself went out with his wife among the so-called artists, went into a room where a lot of them had congregated, he so often got an impression, not of masculine strength and virility, but of something on the whole feminine. Huskier men, fellows like Tom Wills, tried to stay as far away from art talk as they could. Tom Wills never discussed the subject with anyone but Bruce and he hadn't begun doing that until the two men had known each other for several months. There were a lot of other men. Bruce, in his work as a reporter, went about a good deal among gamblers, race-track men, baseball players, prize-fighters, thieves, bootleggers, flash men of all sorts. When he first went to work on the paper he was for a time a sporting writer. On the paper he had a reputation, of a sort. He couldn't write much—never tried. What he could do, Tom Wills thought, was to sense things. It was a faculty of which Bruce did not speak often. Let him be on the track of a murder. Very well, he went into a room where several men were congregated, a bootlegger's place up an alleyway, let us say. He would be willing to bet something that in such a case, if the fellow was hanging around, he could spot the man who had done the job. Proving it was another matter. However, he had the faculty, "the nose for news," it was called among newspaper men. Others had it too.

Oh, Lordy! If he had it, was so almighty keen, why

had he wanted to marry Bernice? He had gone back to his chair by the window, snapping out the light as he went, but now it was quite dark in the street outside. If he had that faculty why had it not worked at a time when surely it was of vital importance to him to have it work?

Again he smiled in the darkness. Now suppose, just suppose now, that I am as much of a nut as Bernice or any of the rest of them. Suppose I am ten times worse. Suppose Tom Wills is ten times worse, too. It might be that I was only a kid when I married Bernice and that I have grown up a little. She thinks I'm a dead one—that I haven't kept up with the show, but, just suppose now, it is she who has dropped behind. I might as well think that. It is a lot more flattering to me than just thinking I'm a chump or that I was a chump when I got married.

BOOK THREE

CHAPTER SEVEN

IT was while thinking some such thoughts that John Stockton, who later became Bruce Dudley, left his wife on a certain fall evening. He sat in the darkness for an hour or two and then got his hat and went out of the house. His physical connection with the apartment in which he had lived with Bernice was slight, a few half-worn neckties hanging on a hook in a closet —three pipes and some shirts and collars in a drawer, two or three suits of clothes, a winter overcoat. Later when he was a workman in the factory at Old Harbor, Indiana, working beside Sponge Martin, hearing Sponge talk, hearing something of the story of Sponge's relations with "his old woman," he hadn't much regret for the way in which he had left. "If you're leaving, one way is as good as another and the less fuss about the matter the better," he told himself. Most of the things Sponge said he had heard before but it was pleasant to hear good talk. The story about that time when Sponge threw the banker out of his carriage-painting shop—let Sponge tell it a thousand times and it would be pleasant to hear. Maybe there was art in that, the grasping of the real dramatic moment of a life, eh? He shrugged his shoulders—thinking. "Sponge, the sawdust pile, the drinks. Sponge coming home drunk in the early morning and finding Bugs, lying on the

[59]

new rag carpet asleep, her arms about the shoulders of
a young man. Bugs, a little live thing, filled with passion—made ugly later—living in a house in Cincinnati
now. Sponge in relation to the town, the Ohio River
Valley, sleeping on an old sawdust pile—his relation to
the ground beneath him, the stars overhead, the brush
in his hand as he painted automobile wheels, the caress
in the hand that held the brush, profanity, crudeness—
love of an old woman—alive like a fox terrier."

What a floating disconnected thing Bruce felt himself. He was a strong man physically. Why had he
never taken hold of life with his hands? Words—the
beginning of poetry, perhaps. The poetry of seed hunger. "I am a seed, floating on a wind. Why have I not
planted myself? Why have I not found ground in
which I can take root?"

Suppose I had come home some evening and walking up to Bernice had struck her a blow. Farmers before planting seed plowed the ground, ripped out old
roots, old weeds. Suppose I had thrown Bernice's
typewriter through a window. "Damn you—no more
driveling words here. Words are tender things, leading to poetry—or lies. Leave craftsmanship to me.
I'm going towards it slowly, carefully, humbly. I'm
a working-man. You get in line and be a working-
man's wife. I'll plow you like a field. I'll harrow
you."

When Sponge Martin talked, telling that story, Bruce
could hear every word said and at the same time go on
having his own thoughts.

That evening when he left Bernice—all his life now

he would be thinking of her vaguely as a thing heard far off—faint determined footsteps crossing a room while he sat looking at the floor and thinking of Tom Wills and of what do you think—oh, Lord, of words. If one couldn't smile at oneself, take a laugh for oneself as one went along, what was the use living at all? Suppose he had gone to Tom Wills that night when he left Bernice. He tried to fancy himself going on a car to the suburbs where Tom lived and knocking on the door. For all he knew Tom had a wife a good deal like Bernice. She might not write stories but at the same time she might be a nut on something—on respectability say.

Suppose, on the night when he left Bernice, Bruce had gone out to Tom Wills' place. Tom's wife coming to the door. "Come in." Then Tom coming in bedroom slippers. Bruce shown into the front room. Bruce remembered that someone down at the newspaper office had once said to him, "Tom Wills' wife is a Methodist."

Just imagine Bruce in that house sitting in the front room with Tom and his wife. "Do you know, I've a notion to leave my wife. Well, you see, she's more interested in other things than in being a woman.

"I just thought I'd come out and tell you folks because I won't be showing up down at the office in the morning. I'm cutting out. To tell the truth I haven't thought much about where I'm going. I'm setting out on a little voyage of discovery. I've a notion that Myself is a land few men know about. I thought I'd take a little trip into myself, look around a little there. God

knows what I'll find. The idea excites me, that's all.
I'm thirty-four and my wife and I have no kids. I
guess I'm a primitive man, a voyager, eh?

> Off again,
> On again,
> Gone again,
> Finnegan.

"Maybe I'll turn out to be a poet."

After Bruce left Chicago, while he wandered south-
ward for some months and later when he worked in the
factory beside Sponge Martin, striving to get from
Sponge something of the workman's quick facility with
his hands, thinking the beginning of education might
lie in a man's relations with his own hands, what he
could do with them, what he could feel with them, what
message they could carry up through his fingers to his
brain, about things, about steel, iron, earth, fire, and
water—while all of this was going on, he amused himself trying to think how he would go at it to tell his
purpose to Tom Wills and his wife—to anyone for
that matter. He thought how amusing it might be to
try to tell Tom and his Methodist wife just all the
thoughts in his head.

He never did go out to Tom and his wife, of course,
and in truth what he actually did had become of minor
importance to Bruce. He had a vague notion that he,
in common with almost all American men, had got out
of touch with things—stones lying in fields, the fields
themselves, houses, trees, rivers, factory walls, tools,
women's bodies, sidewalks, people on sidewalks, men in

overalls, men and women in automobiles. The whole business of the visit to Tom Wills was imagined, an amusing idea to play with as he varnished wheels and Tom Wills had himself become a sort of phantom. He had been replaced by Sponge Martin, by the man actually working beside him. "Perhaps I am a lover of men. That may be why I couldn't stand for the presence of Bernice any more," he thought, smiling at the idea.

There was a certain sum in the bank, some three hundred and fifty dollars, that had been there in his name for a year or two and that he had never told Bernice about. Perhaps he had really intended, from the time he had married her, to do to Bernice some such thing as he finally did. When, as a young man, he left his grandmother's house to go live in Chicago, she had given him five hundred dollars and he had kept three hundred and fifty of it intact. Mighty lucky he did, too, he thought, as he walked about the streets of Chicago that evening after the silent quarrel with the woman. After he left the apartment he went for a walk in Jackson Park and then walked downtown to a cheap hotel and paid two dollars for a room for the night. He slept well enough, and in the morning when he got into the bank at ten he had already found out that there was a train for a town named La Salle, Illinois, at eleven. It was an odd and amusing notion he thought, that one about to go to a town named La Salle, there to buy a second-hand rowboat and start rowing quite casually down a river, leaving a puzzled wife somewhere in the wake of his boat, that such a one should spend the morning playing with the notion of a visit to Tom Wills and his Methodist wife in a house in a suburb.

"And wouldn't his wife have been sore, wouldn t she have given poor Tom a razzing for being the friend of any such casual chap as myself? After all, you see, life is a very serious affair, at least it is when you get it related to somebody else," was what he had thought as he sat on the train—that morning when he left.

CHAPTER EIGHT

FIRST one thing and then another. A liar, an honest man, a thief abruptly slipping out of the service of a daily newspaper in an American city. Newspapers are a necessary part of modern life. They weave the loose ends of life into a pattern. Everyone interested in Leopold and Loeb, the young murderers. All people thinking alike. Leopold and Loeb become the nation's pets. The nation horror-struck about what Leopold and Loeb did. What is Harry Thaw doing now, who is divorced, who fled with the bishop's daughter? Dance life! Awake and dance!

A sneak leaving Chicago on a train at eleven o'clock in the morning, having told his wife nothing of his plans. A woman who has been married misses a man. Living loosely is dangerous—to women. A habit once established is hard to break. Better keep a man around the house. He comes in handy. And then too, for Bernice, the unannounced disappearance of Bruce would be hard to explain. First she would lie. "He had to go out of town for a few days."

Everywhere men trying to explain the actions of their wives, women trying to explain the actions of their husbands. People didn't have to break up homes to get into a position where explanations had to be made. Life should not be as it is. If life were not so complex it would be more simple. I'm sure you would like that kind of a man—if you happen to like that kind of a man, eh?

Bernice would likely enough think Bruce was on a drunk. He had been on two or three royal sprees after he married her. Once he and Tom Wills stayed on a bender for three days and would both have lost their jobs but that it came during Tom's vacation time. Tom saved the reporter's scalp. But never mind that. Bernice might think the paper had sent him out of town.

Tom Wills might phone up to the apartment—a little angry—"Is John sick or what t'ell?"

"No, he was here last night when I went out."

Bernice having her pride hurt. A woman might write short stories, do Sunday special stuff, go about freely with men (modern women who had any sense did that a lot nowdays—it's the mood of the day) "still and all," as that Ring Lardner would say, "it don't make no difference." Women nowdays are putting up a great little fight to get something they want, something they think they want anyway.

That doesn't make them any less women at bottom —maybe it doesn't.

A woman is a special thing then. You got to see that. Wake up, man! Things have changed in the last twenty years. You mossback! If you can get her you get her. If you can't, you can't. Don't you think the world progresses at all? Sure it does. Look at the flying machines we got and the radio. Didn't we have a swell war? Didn't we lick the Germans?

Men want to cheat. That's whereon there is a lot of misunderstanding. What about that three-fifty Bruce kept hidden away for over four years, his getaway stake? When you go to the races, and the meeting lasts, say, thirty days, and you haven't taken a trick and then the meeting is over, how you going to get out of town if you haven't a cent put away, on the quiet? You got to walk out of town or sell the mare, haven't you? Better hide it in the hay.

CHAPTER NINE

THREE or four times after Bruce married Bernice they were both busted higher than a kite. Bernice had to borrow money and so did Bruce. Still and all he said nothing about that three-fifty. Something to the windward, eh? Had he all the time intended just what he finally did? If you're that kind of a cove you might as well smile, get a laugh out of yourself if you can. Pretty soon you'll be dead and then maybe there'll be no laughs. No one ever figured out even Heaven a very jolly place. Dance life! Catch the swing of the dance if you can.

Bruce and Tom Wills used to talk sometimes. They both had the same bees in their bonnets, though the buzzing never came out into words. Just a faint buzzing far off. They talked, tentatively, when they had taken several drinks—about some fellow, an imaginary figure who cut out, left his job, went on the grand sneak. Where to? What for? When they got to that part of their talk both men always felt a little lost. "They raise good apples up in Oregon," Tom said.

"I'm not so apple-hungry," Bruce replied.

Tom had an idea it wasn't only men found life a little dizzy and heavy most of the time, that women had the same feeling—a lot of them anyway. "If they aren't religious or haven't kids there's hell to pay," he said. He told of a woman he knew. "She was a good quiet little wife and went along, tending up to her house, making everything comfortable for her husband, never a word out of her.

"Then something happened. She was pretty good-looking and played the piano pretty well so she got a job playing in a church and after that some fellow who owned a movie theater went to church one Sunday, because his little daughter had died and gone to Heaven the summer before and he felt he ought to square himself when the White Sox weren't playing at home.

"And so he offered her a better job in his movie place. She had a feeling for the keys and was a neat good-looking little thing—or at least a lot of men thought she was." Tom Wills said he didn't think she ever intended it at all, but the first thing you know she began to look down on her husband. "There she was, up on the heights," Tom said. "She took a slant down and began to size up her hubby. He had seemed quite a thing once, but now—it wasn't her fault. After all, young or old, rich or poor, men were pretty easy to get—if you had the touch. She couldn't help it— being talented that way." What Tom meant to say was that this escape hunch was in everyone's bonnet.

Tom never said, "I'd like to beat it myself." He never came out quite that strong. In the newspaper office they said that Tom's wife had something on him. The young Jew who worked there told Bruce once that Tom was scared stiff of his wife, and the next day, when Tom and Bruce were lunching together, Tom told Bruce the same story about the young Jew. The Jew and Tom never got on well together. When Tom came down in the morning and didn't feel very good-natured he always jumped on the Jew. He never did that to Bruce. "A nasty little word-slinger," he said. "He's stuck on himself because he can make words stand on their heads." He leaned over and whispered to Bruce. "Fact," he said, "it happens every Saturday night."

Was Tom nicer to Bruce, did he give him a lot of snap assignments because he thought they were in the same boat?

BOOK FOUR

CHAPTER TEN

HEAT! Bruce Dudley had just come down river. June, July, August, September in New Orleans. You can't make a place something it won't be. It was slow work getting down river. Few or no boats. Often whole days idling about in river towns. You can take a train and go where you please, but what's the hurry?

Bruce at that time, when he had just left Bernice and his newspaper job, had something in mind that expressed itself in the phrase—"What's your hurry?" He sat in the shade of trees by the river-bank, got a ride once on a barge, rode on little local packets, sat in front of stores in river towns, slept, dreamed. People talked with a slow drawling speech, niggers were hoeing cotton, other niggers fished for catfish in the river.

The niggers were something for Bruce to look at, think about. So many black men slowly growing brown. Then would come the light brown, the velvet-browns, Caucasian features. The brown women tending up to the job—getting the race lighter and lighter. Soft Southern nights, warm dusky nights. Shadows flitting at the edge of cotton-fields, in dusky roads by sawmill towns. Soft voices laughing, laughing.

Oh, ma banjo dog,
Oh, ho, ma banjo dog.

• • • • •

An' I ain't go'na give you
None of ma jelly roll.

.   .   .   .   .

So much of that sort of thing in American life. If you are a thinking man—and Bruce was—you make half acquaintances — half friendships — Frenchmen, Germans, Italians, Englishmen—Jews. The Middle Western intellectual circles along the edge of which Bruce had played—watching Bernice plunge more boldly in—were filled with men not American at all. There was a young Polish sculptor, an Italian sculptor, a French dilettante. Was there such a thing as an American? Perhaps Bruce was the thing himself. He was reckless, afraid, bold, shy.

If you are a canvas do you shudder sometimes when the painter stands before you? All the others lending their color to him. A composition being made. Himself the composition.

Could he ever really know a Jew, a German, a Frenchman, an Englishman?

And now a nigger.

Consciousness of brown men, brown women, coming more and more into American life—by that token coming into him too.

More willing to come, more avid to come than any Jew, German, Pole, Italian. Standing laughing—coming by the back door—with shuffling feet, a laugh—a dance in the body.

Facts established would have to be recognized sometime—by individuals—when they were on an intellectual jag perhaps—as Bruce was then.

In New Orleans, when Bruce got there, the long docks facing the river. On the river just ahead of him when he came the last twenty miles, a small houseboat fitted up with a gas engine. Signs on it. "JESUS WILL SAVE." Some itinerant preacher from up river starting south to save the world. "THY WILL BE DONE." The preacher, a sallow man with a dirty beard, in bare feet, at the wheel of the little boat. His wife, also in bare feet, sitting in a rocking-chair. Her teeth were black stumps. Two children in bare feet, lying on a narrow deck.

The docks of the city go around in a great crescent. Big ocean freighters coming in bringing coffee, bananas, fruits, goods, taking out cotton, lumber, corn, oils.

Niggers on the docks, niggers in the city streets, niggers laughing. A slow dance always going on. German sea-captains, French, American, Swedish, Japanese, English, Scotch. The Germans now sailing under other flags than their own. The Scotch sailing under the English flag. Clean ships, dirty tramp ships, half-naked niggers—a shadow-dance.

How much does it cost to be a good man, an earnest man? If we can't produce good earnest men, how are we ever going to make any progress? You can't ever get anywhere if you aren't conscious—in earnest. A brown woman having thirteen children—a different man for every child—going to church too, singing, dancing, broad shoulders, broad hips, soft eyes, a soft laughing voice—getting God on Sunday night—getting —what—on Wednesday night?

Men, you've got to be up and doing if you want progress.

William Allen White, Heywood Broun—passing judgment on the arts—why not—Oh, ma banjo dog—Van Wyck Brooks, Frank Crowninshield, Tululla Bankhead, Henry Mencken, Anita Loos, Stark Young, Ring Lardner, Eva Le Gallienne, Jack Johnson, Bill Heywood, II. G. Wells write good books, don't you think? The Literary Digest, The Dial Book of Modern Art, Harry Wills.

They dance south — out of doors — whites in a pavilion in one field, blacks, browns, high browns, velvet-browns in a pavilion in the next field—but one.

We've got to have more earnest men in this country.

Grass growing in a field between.

Oh, ma banjo dog!

Song in the air, a slow dance. Heat. Bruce had some money then. He might have got a job, but what was the use? Well, he might have gone uptown and tackled the New Orleans *Picayune,* or the *Item* or *States* for a job. Why not go see Jack McClure, the ballad-maker—on the *Picayune?* Give us a song, Jack —a dance—the gumbo drift. Come, the night is hot. What was the use? He still had some of the money he had slipped into his pocket when he left Chicago. In New Orleans you can get a loft in which to sleep for five dollars a month if you know how. You know how when you don't want to work—when you want to look and listen—when you want your body to be lazy while your mind works. New Orleans is not Chicago. It isn't Cleveland or Detroit. Thank God for that!

Nigger girls in the streets, nigger women, nigger men. There is a brown cat lurking in the shadow of a building. "Come, brown puss—come get your cream." The men who work on the docks in New Orleans have slender flanks like running horses, broad shoulders, loose heavy lips hanging down—faces like old monkeys sometimes—bodies like young gods— sometimes. On Sundays—when they go to church, or to a bayou baptizing, the brown girls do sure cut loose with the colors—gaudy nigger colors on nigger women making the streets flame—deep purples, reds, yellows, green like young corn-shoots coming up. They sweat. The skin colors brown, golden yellow, reddish brown, purple-brown. When the sweat runs down high brown backs the colors come out and dance before the eyes. Flash that up, you silly painters, catch it dancing. Song-tones in words, music in words—in colors too. Silly American painters! They chase a Gauguin shadow to the South Seas. Bruce wrote a few poems. Bernice had got very far away in, oh such a short time. Good thing she didn't know. Good thing no one knows how unimportant he is. We need earnest men—got to have 'em. Who'll run the show if we don't get that kind? For Bruce—for the time—no sensual feeling that need be expressed through his body.

Hot days. Sweet Mama!

Funny business, Bruce trying to write poems. When he had that job on the newspaper, where a man is supposed to write, he never wanted to write at all.

Southern white men writing songs—fill themselves first
with Keats and Shelley.

> I am giving out of the richness of myself to many
> mornings.
> At night, when the waters of the seas murmur I am
> murmuring.
> I have surrendered to seas and suns and days and
> swinging ships.
> My blood is thick with surrender.

> It shall be let out through wounds and shall color the
> seas and the earth.
> My blood shall color the earth where the seas come
> for the night kiss and the seas shall be red.

What did that mean? Oh, laugh a little, men!
What matters what it means?

Or again—

> Give me the word.
> Let my throat and my lips caress the words of your lips.

> Give me the word.
> Give me three words, a dozen, a hundred, a history.
> Give me the word.

A broken jargon of words in the head. In old
New Orleans the narrow streets are filled with iron
gates leading away, past damp old walls, to cool patios.
It is very lovely—old shadows dancing on sweet old
walls, but some day it will all be torn away to make
room for factories.

Bruce lived for five months in an old house where

rent was low, where cockroaches scurried up and down the walls. Nigger women lived in the building across the narrow street.

You lie naked on the bed on hot summer mornings and let the slow creeping river-wind come, if it will. Across the street, in another room, a nigger woman of twenty arises at five and stretches her arms. Bruce rolls and looks. Sometimes she sleeps alone but sometimes a brown man sleeps with her. Then they both stretch. Thin-flanked brown man. Nigger girl with slender flexible body. She knows Bruce is looking. What does it matter? He is looking as one might look at trees, at young colts playing in a pasture.

Bruce got out of his bed and went away along a narrow street to another street near the river where he got coffee and a roll of bread for five cents. Thinking of niggers! What sort of business is that? How come? Northern men so often get ugly when they think of niggers, or they get sentimental. Give pity where none is needed. The men and women of the South understand better, maybe. "Oh, hell, don't get fussy! Let things flow! Let us alone! We'll float!" Brown blood flowing, white blood flowing, deep river flowing.

A slow dance, music, ships, cotton, corn, coffee. Slow lazy laughter of niggers. Bruce remembered a line he had once seen written by a negro. "Would white poet ever know why my people walk so softly and laugh at sunrise?"

Heat. The sun coming up in a mustard-colored sky. Driving rains that came, swirled over a half-dozen blocks of city streets and in ten minutes no trace of moisture left. Too much wet warmth for a little more wet warmth to matter. The sun licking it up, taking a drink for itself. One might get clear-headed here. Clear-headed about what? Well, don't hurry. Take your time.

Bruce lay lazy in bed. The brown girl's body was like the thick waving leaf of a young banana plant. If you were a painter now, you could paint that, maybe. Paint a brown nigger girl in a broad leaf waving and send it up North. Why not sell it to a society woman of New Orleans? Get some money to loaf a while longer on. She wouldn't know, would never guess. Paint a brown laborer's narrow suave flanks onto the trunk of a tree. Send it to the Art Institute in Chicago. Send it to the Anderson Galleries in New York. A French painter went down to the South Seas. Freddy O'Brien went down. Remember when the brown woman tried to ravage him and he said how he escaped? Gauguin put a lot of pep in his book but they trimmed it for us. No one cared much, not after Gauguin was dead anyway. You get a cup of such coffee for five cents and a big roll of bread. No swill. In Chicago, morning coffee at cheap places is like swill. Niggers like good things. Good big sweet words, flesh, corn, cane. Niggers like a free throat for song. You're a nigger down South and you get some white blood in you. A little more, and a little more. Northern travelers help, they say. Oh, Lord! Oh, my banjo dog! Do you remember the night when that Gauguin came home to his little hut and there, in the bed, was the slender brown girl waiting for him? Better read that book. "Noa-Noa," they call it. Brown mysticism in the walls of a room, in the hair —of a Frenchman, in the eyes of a brown girl. Noa-Noa. Do you remember the sense of strangeness? French painter kneeling on the floor in the darkness, smelling the strangeness. The brown girl smelling the strangeness. Love? What ho! Smelling strangeness.

Go softly. Don't hurry. What's all the shooting about?

A little more white, a little more white, graying white, muddy white, thick lips—staying sometimes. Over we go!

Something lost too. The dance of bodies, a slow dance.

Bruce on a bed in a five-dollar room. Away off, broad leaves of young banana plants waving. "D'you know why my people laugh in the morning? Do you know why my people walk softly?"

Sleep again, white man. No hurry. Then along a street for coffee and a roll of bread, five cents. Sailors off ships, bleary-eyed. Old nigger women and white women going to market. They know each other, white women, nigger women. Go soft. Don't hurry!

Song—a slow dance. A white man lying still on docks, in a five-dollar-a-month bed. Heat. No hurry. When you get that hurry out of you the mind works maybe. Maybe song will start in you too.

Lord, it would be nice with Tom Wills down here.

Shall I write him a letter? No, better not. After a while, when cool days come, you mosey along up North again. Come back here some day. Stay here some day. Look and listen.

Song—dance—a slow dance.

BOOK FIVE

CHAPTER ELEVEN

"SATURDAY night and supper on the table. My old woman cooking supper—what! Me with a pipe in my mouth."

> Lif' up the skillet, put down the lid,
> Mama's go'na make me some a-risen bread.
>
> .   .   .   .   .
>
> An' I ain't go'na give you
> None of my jelly roll.
>
> An' I ain't go'na give you
> None of my jelly roll.
>
> .   .   .   .   .

Saturday evening in the factory at Old Harbor. Sponge Martin putting his brushes away and Bruce imitating his every movement. "Leave the brushes so and they'll be fine and fit on Monday morning."

Sponge singing as he puts things away, clears up. An orderly little cuss—Sponge. He's got the workman's instinct. Likes things so and so, tools in order.

"Messy men make me sick. I hate 'em."

The surly man who worked next to Sponge was in a great hurry to get out at the door. He had been ready to leave for ten minutes.

No cleaning up brushes, putting things in order for

him. Every two minutes he looked at his watch. His hurry amused Sponge.

"Wants to get home and see if his old woman is still there—alone. He wants to go home and don't want to go. If he loses her he's afraid he'll never get another woman. Women are so damned hard to get. They haint hardly any left. Only about ten million of 'em around loose—without any man—specially in New England, I've heard," Sponge said, winking as the surly workman hurried away without saying good-night to his two fellows.

Bruce had a suspicion that Sponge had made up the story about the workman and his wife to amuse himself, to amuse Bruce.

He and Sponge went out at the door together. "Why don't you come on down for Sunday dinner?" Sponge said. He invited Bruce every Saturday night, and Bruce had already accepted several times.

Now he walked beside Sponge up a climbing street toward his hotel, a small working-man's hotel, on a street half-way up the Old Harbor hill, a hill that climbed abruptly up almost from the river's edge. At the river's edge, on a shelf of land just above the high-water line, there was only room for a line of railroad tracks and for the row of factory buildings between the tracks and the river's edge. Across the tracks and a narrow road by the factory doors, streets climbed up the side of the hill and other streets ran parallel with the tracks around the hill. The business section of the town was almost half-way up the hillside.

The long red-brick buildings of the wheel company,

then a dusty road, the railroad tracks and after that clusters of streets of working-men's houses, small frame affairs close together, then two streets of stores, and above the beginning of what Sponge called "the swell part of town."

The hotel where Bruce lived was in a street of working-men's houses, just above the business streets, "half swell and half low-life," Sponge said.

Time was—when Bruce, then John Stockton, was a lad and lived for a time at the same hotel—that it was in the "swellest" part of town. The land running on up the hill was pretty much country then, with trees covering the hill. Before automobiles came, it was too much work getting up the hill and besides Old Harbor hadn't many swells. That was when his father had got the job as principal in the high school at Old Harbor and just before the little family went to live in Indianapolis.

Bruce, then in knee-pants, with his father and mother, had lived in two adjoining rooms—small ones on the second floor of the three-storied frame hotel. It wasn't the best hotel in town, even then, nor was it what it had now become—half a laborers' rooming-house.

The hotel was still owned by the same woman, a widow, who had owned it when Bruce was a boy. Then she was a young widow with two children, a boy and a girl—the boy two or three years the older. He had disappeared from the scene when Bruce came back there to live—had gone to Chicago where he had a job as copy-writer in an advertising agency. Bruce had grinned when he heard of that. "Lordy, a kind of circle of life. You start somewhere, come back to where you started. It doesn't much matter what your intentions are. Round and round you go. Now you see it and now you don't." His Dad and that kid both working at the same job in Chicago, crossing each other's tracks, both in earnest about their jobs, too. When he heard what the son of the house was doing in Chicago, there popped into Bruce's mind a story one of the boys in the newspaper office had told him. It was a story about certain people, Iowa people, Illinois people, Ohio people. The Chicago newspaper man had seen a lot of people when he went for a trip with a friend in a car. "They are in business or they own a farm and suddenly they begin to feel they aren't getting anywhere. Then they sell the little farm or the store and buy a Ford. They start traveling, men, women and kids. Out they go to California and get tired of that. They move on down to Texas and then to Florida. The car rattles and bangs like a milk-wagon but they keep on the go. Finally they get back to where they started and then begin the whole show all over again. The country is getting all filled up with such caravans, thousands of them. When such an out-fit goes broke they settle down wherever they happen to be, become farm-hands or factory-hands. There's a lot of them. It's the American passion for being on the go, a little going to seed, I guess."

The son of the widow who owned the hotel had gone off to Chicago and had got a job and married, but the daughter hadn't had any such luck. She hadn't found herself a man. Now the mother was getting old and the daughter was slipping into her place. The hotel had changed because the town had changed. When Bruce was a kid, living there in knee-pants with his father and mother, several half-important people— like his father, the principal in the high school, a young unmarried doctor and two young lawyers—lived there. Traveling men who wanted to save a little money did not go to the more expensive hotel on the chief business street, but were satisfied with the neat little place on the hillside above. In the evening, when Bruce was a child, such men used to sit in chairs before the hotel talking, explaining to each other their presence in the less expensive place. "I like it. It's quieter up here," one of them said. They were trying to make a little money on their travelers' expense accounts and seemed half ashamed of the fact.

The daughter of the house was then a pretty little thing with long yellow curls. On spring and fall evenings she was always playing about the front of the hotel. The traveling men petted and fussed with her and she liked it. One by one they took her to sit in their laps and gave her pennies or sticks of candy. "How long had that lasted?" Bruce wondered. At what age had she become self-conscious, a woman? Perhaps she had slid off one thing and into another without knowing. One evening she had been sitting on the knees of a young man and suddenly she had a feeling. She didn't know what it was. It wasn't proper for her to do that sort of thing any more. Down she jumped and walked away with a certain dignified air that made the traveling men and others sitting about laugh. The young traveling man tried to get her to come back and sit on his lap again but she wouldn't and then she went into the hotel and up to her room feeling—Lord knows what.

Did that happen when Bruce was a child there? He, his father and mother used to go sit in the chairs before the door of the hotel sometimes on spring and fall evenings. His father's position in the high school gave him a certain dignity in the eyes of the others.

And what about Bruce's mother, Martha Stockton. It was odd what a distinct, and at the same time indistinct figure she had been to him since he had grown to manhood. He had all sorts of dreams about her, thoughts about her. Now sometimes, in the life of his fancy, she was young and handsome, and sometimes she was old and tired of life. Had she become merely a figure his fancy played with? A mother, after her death, or after you no longer live near her, is something the male fancy can play with, dream of, make a part of the movement of the grotesque dance of life. Idealize her. Why not? She is gone. She will not come near to break the thread of the dream. The dream is as true as the reality. Who knows the difference? Who knows anything?

> Mother, dear mother, come home to me now
> The clock in the steeple strikes ten.

.   .   .   .   .

> Silver threads among the gold.

Sometimes Bruce wondered if the same thing had happened to his father's conception of the dead woman that had happened to his own. When he and his father lunched together in Chicago he had sometimes wanted to ask the older man questions but dared not. It might have been done perhaps if there hadn't been that feeling between Bernice and his father's new wife. Why had they taken such a dislike to each other? It would have been worth while to have been able to say to the older man: "What about it, eh, Dad? Which do you most like having near you—the living body of the younger woman or the half real, half manufactured dream of the one who died?" A mother's figure, held in solution—in a floating, changing liquid thing—the fancy.

The flashy young Jew in the newspaper office could sure sling great mother stuff—"gold-star mothers sending sons off to war—the mother of a young murderer in court—in black—put in there by the son's attorney —a fox, that fellow—good jury stuff." When Bruce was a child he, with his mother and father, lived on the same floor of the hotel at Old Harbor where he later got a room. Then there was the room for his father and mother and the smaller one for himself. The bathroom was on the same floor several doors away. Perhaps the place looked then much as it did now, but to Bruce it seemed infinitely more shabby. On the day when he came back to Old Harbor and went to the hotel, and when he was shown to a room, he trembled, thinking the woman who led the way upstairs for him was about to lead him to the same room. At first, when he was left alone in the room, he thought it might be the same one he had occupied as a child. His mind went, "click, click," like an old clock in an empty house. "Oh, Lord! Ring around the rosy, eh?" Gradually things cleared. He decided it wasn't the same room. He wouldn't have it be the same.

"Better not. I might wake up some night, crying for mother, wanting her soft arms about me, my head on her soft breasts. Mother-complex—something of that sort. I'm supposed to be trying to cut loose from memories. Get some new breath into my nostrils if I can. The dance of life! Don't stop. Don't go back. Dance the dance out to the end. Listen, do you hear the music?"

The woman who had shown him to the room was undoubtedly the child of the curls. That he knew by her name. She had grown a little stout, but wore neat clothes. Her hair was already a little gray. Was she, inside herself, still a child? Did he want to be a child again? Was that what had drawn him back to Old Harbor? "Well, hardly," he had said to himself, stoutly. "I'm on another lay just now."

But, about that woman, the hotel woman's daughter—herself now a hotel woman?

Why hadn't she got her a man? Perhaps she hadn't wanted one. It might be that she had seen too much of men. He, himself, as a child, had never played with the two hotel children because the little girl had made him feel shy when he met her alone in the halls and because, as the boy was two or three years older, he felt shy with him too.

In the morning, when he was a child in knee-trousers, living in the hotel with his father and mother, he went off to school walking usually with his father, and in the afternoon, when school was out, came home alone. His father stayed at the schoolhouse until later, correcting papers or something of that sort.

In the late afternoon and when the weather was fine Bruce and his mother went for a walk. What had she been doing all day? There was no food to cook. They dined in the hotel dining-room among the traveling men and the farmers and town people who came there to eat. A few business men also came. Supper then was twenty-five cents. A procession of strange people always passing in and out of a boy's fancy. Plenty of things for the fancy to feed on then. Bruce had been a rather silent boy. His mother was that type too. Bruce's father did the talking for the family.

What did his mother do all day? She did a lot of sewing. Also she made lace. Later, when Bruce married Bernice, his grandmother, with whom he had lived after his mother died, sent her a lot of lace the mother had made. It was rather delicate stuff, turned a little yellow with age. Bernice was glad to get it. She wrote a note to the grandmother saying how sweet it was of her to send it.

In the afternoon, when the lad, who was now a man of thirty-four, got home from school, about four, his mother took him for a walk. At that time several river packets came regularly to Old Harbor and both the woman and her child liked to go down to the levee. What a bustle! What a singing, swearing and shouting! The town, that had been sleeping all day in the heat of the river valley, suddenly awoke. Drays drove pell-mell down the hillside streets, there was a cloud of dust, dogs barked, boys ran and shouted, a whirlwind of energy swept over the town. It seemed a life-and-death matter that the boat not be kept at the landing an unnecessary moment. The boats landed goods and took on and put off passengers near a street of small stores and saloons that stood on the ground now occupied by the Grey Wheel Factory. The stores faced the river and at their back doors ran the railroad that was slowly but surely choking the river life to death. What an unromantic thing the railroad seemed, there in sight of the river and the river life.

Bruce's mother took her child down the sloping streets to one of the small stores facing the river where she usually bought some trifle, a package of pins or needles or a spool of thread. Then she and the boy sat on a bench before the store and the storekeeper came to the door to speak to her. He was a neat-looking man with a gray mustache. "The boy likes looking at the boats and the river, doesn't he, Mrs. Stockton?" he said. The man and the woman talked of the heat of the late September day or of the chances for rain. Then a customer appeared and the man disappeared inside the store and did not come out again. The boy knew his mother had bought the trifle in the store because she didn't like to sit on the bench in front without giving the store a little patronage. Already that part of town was going to pieces. The business of the town was drawing away from the river, had turned its back on the river where all the town life had once centered.

The woman and the boy sat for an hour on the
bench. The light began to soften and a cool evening
breeze blew up the river valley. How seldom the
woman spoke! It was sure Bruce's mother had not
been very social. The wife of the principal of the
school could have had a good many women friends in
the town but she did not seem to want them. Why?

When a boat was coming in or going out it was
very exciting. There was a long broad landing-plank
that had been let down on the sloping levee, into which
cobblestones had been set, and niggers ran or trotted
on and off the boat with loads on their heads or shoulders. They were barefooted and often half naked.
On hot days in the late May or early September how
their black faces, backs and shoulders shone in the
afternoon light! There was the boat, the slowly moving gray waters of the river, the green of the trees over
on the Kentucky shore and the woman sitting beside the
boy—so near and yet so far away.

Certain things, impressions, pictures, memories had
got fixed in the boy's mind. They stayed there after
the woman was dead and he had himself become a man.

The woman. Mystery. Love of women. Scorn of
women. What are they like? Are they like trees?
How much can woman thrust into the mystery of life,
think, feel? Love men. Take women. Drift with the
drifting of days. That life goes on does not concern
you. It concerns women.

Thoughts of a man dissatisfied with life, as it had
presented itself to him confused with what he thought
a boy had felt sitting by a river with a woman. Be-

fore he got old enough to be at all conscious of her, as a being like himself, she died. Had he, Bruce, in the years after she died and while he was growing to manhood and after he became a grown man, had he manufactured the feeling he had come to have concerning her? That might be. It might be he had done it because Bernice did not seem much of a mystery.

The lover must love. It is his nature. Did men like Sponge Martin, who were workmen and lived and felt down through their fingers—did they get life more clearly?

Bruce walking out at a factory door with Sponge on a Saturday evening. Winter almost gone, spring coming soon now.

Before the factory door at the wheel of an automobile a woman—the wife of Grey, the owner of the factory. Another woman sitting on a bench beside her boy looking at the moving face of a river in the evening light. Drifting thoughts, fancies in a man's mind. The reality of life clouded at the moment. Seed-sowing hunger, soil-hunger. A group of words caught in the meshes of the mind drifting up into consciousness, forming words on his lips. As Sponge talked, Bruce and the woman in the car, for a moment only, looked into each other's eyes.

The words in Bruce's mind at the moment were from the Bible. "And Judah said unto Onan, Go in unto thy brother's wife, and marry her, and raise up seed to thy brother."

What a queer jumble of words—ideas. Bruce had been away from Bernice for several months. Was he on the lookout for another woman now? Why the startled look in the eyes of the woman in the automobile? Had he embarrassed her by staring at her? But she had stared at him. There had been a look in her eyes as though she were about to speak to him, a workman in her husband's factory. He would listen to Sponge.

Bruce walked beside Sponge without looking back. "What a thing that Bible!" It had been one of the few books Bruce never tired of reading. When he was a boy and after his mother died his grandmother always had the book about—reading in the New Testament, but he read the older Testament. Stories— men and women in relation to each other—fields, sheep, grain growing, famine coming into a land, years of plenty coming. Joseph, David, Saul, Samson, the strong man — honey, bees, barns, cattle — men and women going into barns to lie on the threshing-floors. "When he saw her—he thought her to be a harlot because she had covered her face." That was when he went up unto his sheep-shearers to Timorath, he and his friend Hirah, the Adullamite.

"And he turned unto her by the way and said, Go to, I pray thee, let me come in unto you."

And why had not that young Jew in the newspaper office in Chicago read the book of his fathers? There would not have been such loose word-slinging then.

Sponge on a sawdust pile in the Ohio River Valley beside his old woman—the old woman who was alive like a fox terrier.

A woman in an automobile with her eyes on Bruce.

A workman, like Sponge, saw, felt, tasted things through his fingers. There was a disease of life due to men getting away from their own hands, their own bodies too. Things felt with the whole body—rivers —trees—skies—grasses growing—grain growing— ships—seed stirring in the ground—city streets—dust in city streets—steel—iron—sky-scrapers—faces in city streets—bodies of men—bodies of women— children's quick slender bodies.

That young Jew in the Chicago newspaper office slinging words brilliantly—slinging the bunk. Bernice writing that story about the poet and the woman of wax, Tom Wills swearing at the young Jew. "He's afraid of his woman."

Bruce cutting out from Chicago—spending weeks on a river—on the docks in New Orleans.

Thoughts of his mother — thoughts of a boy's thoughts of his mother. A man like Bruce could think a hundred diverse thoughts walking ten steps beside a workman named Sponge Martin.

Had Sponge noticed the little passage between him-self—Bruce—and that woman in the car? He had felt it—perhaps through his fingers.

"That woman's taken a shine to you. Better look out," Sponge said.

Bruce smiled.

More thoughts of his mother as he walked with Sponge. Sponge talking. He did not press the theme of the woman in the car. It might just have been a workman's slant. Workmen were like that, they thought of women only in one way. There was a kind of terrible matter-of-factness about workmen. More than likely most of their observations were lies. De diddle de dum dum! De diddle de dum dum!

Bruce remembered, or thought he remembered, certain things about his mother, and after he came back to Old Harbor they piled up in his consciousness. The nights in the hotel. After the evening meal and when the nights were fair he, with his father and mother, sat about with the strangers, travelers and others, before the door of the hotel and then Bruce was put to bed. Sometimes the principal of the school got into a discussion with some man. "Is a protective tariff a good thing? Don't you think it will raise prices too much? The fellow between will get crushed between the upper and the nether millstone."

What was a nether millstone?

The father and mother went to sit in their rooms, the man reading school papers and the woman a book. Sometimes she worked at her sewing. Then the woman came into the boy's room and kissed him on both cheeks. "Now you go to sleep," she said. Sometimes after he was in bed the parents went out for a walk. Where did they go? Did they go to sit on the bench by the tree in front of the store on the street facing the river?

The river going on always—a huge thing. It never seemed to hurry. After a while it joined another river, called the Mississippi, and went away south. More and more water flowing. When he was lying in bed the river seemed to flow through the boy's head. On spring nights, sometimes, when the man and woman were out, there came a sudden flaw of rain and he got out of his bed and went to the open window. The sky was dark and mysterious, but when one looked down from his second-story room there was the cheerful sight of people going hurriedly along a street, going downhill along a street toward the river, dodging in and out of doorways to avoid the rain.

On other nights in bed there was just the dark space where the window and the sky were. Men passed along a hallway outside his door—traveling men going to bed—heavy-footed fat men, most of them.

The man Bruce had somehow got his notion of his mother mixed up with his feeling about the river. He was quite conscious that it was all rather a muddle in his head. Mother Mississippi, Mother Ohio, eh? That was all tommyrot, of course. "Poetic bunk," Tom Wills would have called it. It was symbolism, getting off your base, saying one thing and meaning another. Still there might be something in it—something Mark Twain had almost got and didn't dare try to quite get —the beginning of a kind of big continental poetry, eh? Warm, big rich rivers flowing down—Mother Ohio, Mother Mississippi. When you begin to get smart you got to look out for that kind of bunk. Go easy, brother, if you say it out loud some foxy city man may laugh at you. Tom Wills growling, "Ah, cut it out!" When you were a boy and sat looking at the river something appeared, a dark spot away off up river. You watched it coming slowly down but it was so far out that you could not see what it was. Water-soaked logs sometimes bobbed along, just one end sticking up like a man swimming. It might be a swimmer away out there but of course it couldn't be. Men do not swim down the Ohio, miles and miles, down the Mississippi, miles and miles. When Bruce was a child and sat on the bench watching, he half closed his eyes, and his mother sitting beside him did the same thing. The thing to figure out later, when he was a grown man, was whether or not he and his mother had, at the same time, the same thoughts. Perhaps the thoughts Bruce later fancied he had, as a child, hadn't come at all. The fancy was a tricky thing. What one was trying to do with the fancy was to link oneself, in some rather mysterious way, with others.

You watched the log bob along. Now it was opposite you, away over near the Kentucky shore where the slow strong current was.

And now it would begin to get smaller and smaller. How long could you keep it in sight, on the gray face of the waters, a little black thing getting smaller and smaller? It became a test. The need was terrible. What need? To keep the eyes glued on a drifting, floating black spot on a moving surface of yellow-gray, to hold the eyes there fixed, as long as possible.

What did a man or woman sitting on a bench on a street on a dusky evening and looking at the darkening face of a river, what did they see? Why had they need to do the rather absurd thing together? When the child's father and mother were out alone together at night was there something of the same kind of need in them? Did they meet the need in such a childish way? When they came home and had got into bed sometimes they talked in low tones and sometimes they were silent.

CHAPTER TWELVE

OTHER strange memories for Bruce, walking with Sponge. When he went with his father and mother from Old Harbor to Indianapolis they went by boat to Louisville. Then Bruce was twelve. His memories of that occasion might be more trustworthy. They got up in the early morning and went in a hack to the boat-landing. There were two other passengers, two young men who were evidently not citizens of Old Harbor. Who were they? Certain figures, seen under certain circumstances, remain sharply in the memory always. A tricky business though, taking such things too seriously. It might lead to mysticism and an American mystic would be something ridiculous.

That woman in the car by the factory door Bruce and Sponge had just passed. Odd that Sponge had known about there being a passage—of a sort—between her and Bruce. He hadn't been looking.

Odd, too, if Bruce's mother had been one who was always making such contacts, making them and her man—Bruce's father—not knowing.

She, herself, might not have known—not consciously.

That day of his boyhood on the river had undoubtedly been very vivid to Bruce.

To be sure, Bruce was a child then, and to a child the adventure of going to live at a new place is something tremendous.

What will be seen at the new place, what people will be there, what will life be like there?

The two young men who had got on the boat that morning when he, with his father and mother, left Old Harbor, had stood by a railing on an upper deck talking while the boat got out into the stream. One was rather heavy, a broad-shouldered man with black hair and big hands. He smoked a pipe. The other was slender and had a small black mustache which he kept stroking.

Bruce sat with his father and mother on a bench. The morning passed. Landings were made and goods were put off the boat. The two young men passengers kept walking about, laughing and talking earnestly, and the child had a feeling that one of them, the slender man, had some sort of connection with his mother. It was as though the man and the woman had once known each other and now were embarrassed finding themselves on the same boat. When they passed the bench where the Stocktons sat the slender man did not look at them but out over the river. Bruce had a shy boyish desire to call to him. He became absorbed in the young man and in his mother. How young she looked that day—like a girl.

Bruce's father got into a long talk with the captain of the boat who bragged of his experiences in the early days on the river. He talked of the black deck-hands, "We owned them then, like so many horses, but we had to take care of them like horses. It was after the war we began getting the most out of them. They were our property just the same, do you see, but we couldn't sell them and we could always get all we wanted. Niggers love the river. You can't keep a nigger off the river. We used to get 'em for five or six dollars a month and we didn't pay 'em that if we didn't want to. Why should we? If a nigger got gay we knocked him into the river. No one ever made any inquiry about a missing nigger, them days."

The boat-captain and the school-teacher went away to another part of the boat and Bruce sat alone with his mother. In his memory—after she died—she remained a slender, rather small woman with a sweet, serious face. Almost always she was quiet and reserved, but sometimes—rarely—as on that day on the boat she became strangely alive and eager. In the afternoon when the boy had grown tired running about the boat he went to sit with her again. Evening came. Within an hour they would be tied up at Louisville. The captain had taken Bruce's father up into the pilot-house. Near Bruce and his mother stood the two young men. The boat came to a landing, the last landing it would make before reaching the city.

There was a long sloping shore with cobblestones set in the mud of the river levee and the town at which they had stopped was much like the town of Old Harbor, only somewhat smaller. Many bags of grain were to be put off and the niggers were trotting up and down the landing-stage singing as they worked.

From the throats of the ragged black men as they trotted up and down the landing-stage, strange haunting notes. Words were caught up, tossed about, held in the throat. Word-lovers, sound-lovers—the blacks seemed to hold a tone in some warm place, under their red tongues perhaps. Their thick lips were walls under which the tone hid. Unconscious love of inanimate things lost to the whites—skies, the river, a moving boat—black mysticism—never expressed except in song or in the movements of bodies. The bodies of the black workers belonged to each other as the sky belonged to the river. Far off now, down river, where the sky was splashed with red, it touched the face of the river. The tones from the throats of the black workers touched each other, caressed each other. On the deck of the boat a red-faced mate stood swearing as though at the sky and the river.

The words coming from the throats of the black workers could not be understood by the boy but were strong and lovely. Afterwards when he thought of that moment Bruce always remembered the singing voices of the negro deck-hands as colors. Streaming reds, browns, golden yellows coming out of black throats. He grew strangely excited inside himself, and his mother, sitting beside him, was also excited. "Ah, my baby! Ah, my baby!" Sounds caught and held in black throats. Notes split into quarter-notes. The word, as meaning, of no importance. Perhaps words were always unimportant. There were strange words about a "banjo dog." What was a "banjo dog?" "Ah, my banjo dog! Oh, oh! Oh, oh! Ah, my banjo dog!"

Brown bodies trotting, black bodies trotting. The

bodies of all the men running up and down the landing-stage were one body. One could not be distinguished from another. They were lost in each other.

Could the bodies of people be so lost in each other? Bruce's mother had taken the boy's hand and held it closely, warmly. Near by stood the slender young man who had got on the boat in the morning. Did he know how the mother and the boy felt at that moment and did he want to be a part of them? There was no doubt that all day, as the boat labored up river, there had been something between the woman and the man, something of which they had both been but semi-conscious. The school-teacher had not known, but the boy and the slender young man's companion had known. Long after that evening sometimes—thoughts coming into the head of a man who had once been a boy on a boat with his mother. All day as the man had gone about the boat he had talked to his companion but there had been a call in him toward the woman with the child. Something within him went toward the woman as the sun went toward the western horizon.

Now the evening sun seemed to be about to drop into the river, far off to the west, and the sky was rosy red.

The young man's hand rested on the shoulder of his companion but his face was turned toward the woman and the child. The woman's face was red, like the evening sky. She did not look at the young man, but away from him across the river and the boy looked from the young man's face to his mother's face. His mother's hand gripped his hand tightly.

Bruce never had any brothers or sisters. Could it be that his mother had wanted more children? Long afterwards, sometimes—that time after he left Bernice, when he was floating down the Mississippi River in an open boat, before he lost his boat one night in a storm when he had gone ashore—odd things happened. He pulled the boat ashore under a tree somewhere and lay down on the grass on the river-bank. An empty river filled with ghosts before his eyes. He was half asleep, half awake. Fancies flooded his mind. Before the storm came that blew his boat away he lay for a long time in the darkness near the water's edge reliving another evening on a river. The strangeness and the wonder of things—in nature—he had known as a boy and that he had somehow later lost—the sense lost living in a city and being married to Bernice—could he get it back again? There was the strangeness and wonder of trees, skies, city streets, black men, white men— of buildings, words, sounds, thoughts, fancies. Perhaps white men's getting on so fast in life, having newspapers, advertising, great cities, smart clever minds, ruling the world, had cost them more than they had gained. They hadn't gained much.

That young man Bruce had once seen on an Ohio river-boat when he was a boy taking the trip up river with his father and mother—had he on that evening been something of what Bruce later became? It would be an odd turn of the mind if the young man had never existed—if a boy's mind had invented him. Suppose he had just invented him later—as something—to explain his mother to himself as a means for getting close to the woman, his mother. The man's memory of the woman, his mother, might also be an invention. A mind like Bruce's sought explanations for everything.

On the boat on the Ohio River, evening coming on fast. There was a town sitting high up on a bluff and three or four people had got off the boat. The niggers kept singing—singing and trotting—dancing up and down a landing-stage. A broken-down hack, to which two decrepit-looking horses were hitched, went away up along a street toward the town on the bluff. On the shore were two white men. One was small and alert and had an account-book in his hand. He was checking off the grain-bags as they were brought ashore. "One-hundred-twenty-two, twenty-three, twenty-four." "Ah, my banjo dog! Oh, ho! Oh, ho!"

The second white man on the shore was tall and lean and there was something wild about his eyes. On the still evening air the voice of the captain of the boat, talking to Bruce's father up above in the pilot-house or on the deck above, could be distinctly heard. "He's a crazy man." The second white man ashore sat at the top of the levee with his knees drawn up between his arms. His body rocked slowly to and fro in the rhythm of the singing negroes. The man had been in some kind of an accident. There was a cut on his long lean cheek and the blood had run down into his dirty beard and dried there. There was a tiny streak of red faintly seen like the streak of fiery red in the red sky of the west the boy could see when he looked away down river toward the setting sun. The injured man was dressed in ragged clothes and his lips hung open, thick lips hanging open like niggers' lips when they sang. His body rocked. The body of the slender young man on the boat, who was trying to keep up a conversation with his companion, the broad-shouldered man, was rocking almost imperceptibly. The body of the woman who was Bruce's mother was rocking.

To the boy on the boat that evening the whole world, the sky, the boat, the shore running away into the gathering darkness seemed rocking with the voices of the singing niggers.

Had the whole thing been but a fancy, a whim? Had he, as a boy, gone to sleep on a boat with his hand gripped in his mother's hand and dreamed it all? It had been hot all day on the narrow-decked river-boat. The gray waters running along beside the boat made a boy sleepy.

What had happened between a small woman sitting silently on the deck of a boat and a young man with a tiny mustache who talked all day to his friend, never addressing a word to the woman? What could happen between people that no one knew anything about, that they themselves knew little about?

As Bruce walked beside Sponge Martin and passed a woman sitting in an automobile and something—a flashing kind of thing passed between them—what did it signify?

On the boat, that day on the river, Bruce's mother had turned her face toward the young man, even as the boy watched the two faces. It was as though she had suddenly consented to something—a kiss perhaps.

No one had known but the boy and perhaps—as a wild fanciful notion—the crazy man sitting on the river levee and staring at the boat—his thick lips hanging open. "He's three-quarters white and one-quarter nigger, and he's been crazy for ten years," the voice of the captain explained to the school-teacher on the deck above.

The crazy man sat hunched up ashore, on the top of the levee, until the boat was pulling away from the landing and then he got to his feet and shouted. Later the captain said he did it whenever a boat landed at the town. The man was harmless, the captain said. The crazy man with the streak of red blood on his cheek got to his feet and stood up very straight and tall. His body seemed like the trunk of a dead tree growing at the levee-top. There might have been a dead tree there. The boy might have gone to sleep and dreamed it all. He had been strangely attracted to the slender young man. He might have wanted the young man near himself and had let his fancy draw him near through the body of a woman, his mother.

.   .   .   .   .

How ragged and dirty were the clothes of the crazy man! A kiss had passed between the young woman on deck and the slender young man. The crazy man shouted something. "Keep afloat! Keep afloat!" he cried, and all the niggers down below on the lower deck of the boat were silent. The body of the young man with the mustache quivered. A woman's body quivered. A boy's body quivered.

"All right," the captain's voice shouted. "It's all right. We'll take care of ourselves."

"He's just a harmless lunatic, comes down every time a boat comes in and always shouts something like that," the captain explained to Bruce's father as the boat swung out into the stream.

CHAPTER THIRTEEN

SATURDAY night and supper on the table. The old woman cooking supper—what!

> Lif' up the skillet, put down the lid,
> Mama's go'na make me some a-risen bread!
> .   .   .   .   .
>
> An' I ain't go'na give you none of my jelly roll.
> An' I ain't go'na give you none of my jelly roll.
> .   .   .   .   .

A Saturday evening in the early spring in Old Harbor, Indiana. In the air the first faint promise of the hot moist summer days to come. In the lowlands up and down river from Old Harbor the river flood-waters still covered the deep flat fields. A warm rich land of growth—trees growing rank—woods and corn growing rank. The whole Middle American empire—swept by frequent and delicious rains, great forests, prairies on which early spring flowers grow like a carpet— land of many rivers running down to the brown slow strong mother of rivers, land to live in, make love in, dance in. Once the Indians danced there, made feasts there. They threw poems about like seeds on a wind. Names of rivers, names of towns. Ohio! Illinois! Keokuk! Chicago! Illinois! Michigan!

On Saturday evening when Sponge and Bruce put

away their brushes and came out of the factory, Sponge
kept urging Bruce to come to his house for Sunday
dinner. "You ain't got no old woman. My old woman
likes to have you there."

Sponge was in a playful mood, Saturday evening.
On Sunday he would stuff himself with fried chicken,
mashed potatoes, chicken gravy, pie. Then he would
stretch himself on the floor beside his front door and
sleep. If Bruce came he would manage in some way
to get a bottle of whisky and Sponge would have
several long pulls at the bottle. After Bruce had taken
a pull or two Sponge and his old woman would finish
it. Then the old woman would sit in a rocking-chair,
laughing and teasing Sponge. "He ain't much good
any more—not much juice in him. I got to be looking
out for a younger man—like you maybe," she said,
winking at Bruce. Sponge laughed and rolled on the
floor, grunting sometimes, like a fat clean old pig. "I
got you two kids. What's got wrong with you?"

"Time now to think of going fishing—some pay-day
night—soon now, eh, old woman?"

On the table the dishes unwashed. The two older
people slept. Sponge with his body across the open
door, the old woman in her rocking-chair. Her mouth
fell open. She had false teeth in the upper jaw. Flies
came in at the open door and settled on the table. Feed,
flies! Plenty of fried chicken left, plenty of gravy,
plenty of mashed potatoes.

Bruce had an idea the dishes were left unwashed because Sponge wanted to help clear up, but neither he
nor the old woman wanted another man to see him

helping do a woman's task. Bruce could imagine a conversation between them before he came. "Look here, old woman, you let them dishes alone. You wait 'til later, 'til after he goes."

Sponge owned an old brick house that had once been a stable near the river's edge where the stream bent away to the north. The railroad ran past his kitchen door, and in front of his house, down nearer the water's edge, there was a dirt road. In the spring floods, sometimes, the road was under water and Sponge had to wade in water to get up to the tracks.

In an earlier day the dirt road had been the main road into the town and there had been a tavern and a stage-coach station, but the small brick stable Sponge had bought at a low price and had converted into a house—when he was a young man and had just got him a wife—was the only indication of former grandeur left along the road.

Five or six hens and a rooster walked in the road that was full of deep ruts. Few automobiles came that way and when the others slept Bruce stepped carefully over Sponge's body and walked away from town along the road. When he had gone a half-mile and had left the town behind, the road turned away from the river into the hills and, just at that point, the current set in sharp against the river-bank. The road there was in danger of falling into the river and at this point Bruce loved to sit on a log near the river's edge and look down. There was a fall of perhaps ten feet and the current was eating and eating at the banks. Logs and driftwood carried by the current almost touched the shore and then were carried out again into the middle of the stream.

It was a place to sit, dreaming and thinking. When he grew tired of the sight of the river he went into the hill country, returning to town in the evening by a new road directly over the hills.

Sponge in the shop just before the time when the whistle blew on Saturday afternoon. He was a man who had spent all the years of his life working and eating and sleeping. When Bruce had worked on the newspaper in Chicago he had gone out of the newspaper office in the afternoon feeling dissatisfied, empty. Often he and Tom Wills went to sit in some dark little restaurant on a side street. There was a place just over the river on the North Side where bootleg whisky and wine could be had. For two or three hours they sat drinking in the little dark place while Tom growled.

"What a life for a grown man—throwing bunk— sending others out to gather up city scandal—the Jew dressing it up in gaudy words."

Although he was old Sponge did not seem tired when the day's work was done but as soon as he got home and had eaten he wanted to sleep. All afternoon, on Sunday, after the Sunday dinner, at noon, he slept. Was the man entirely satisfied with life? Did his job satisfy him, his wife, the house in which he lived, the bed in which he slept? Did he have no dreams, seek nothing he could not find? When he awoke on a summer morning after a night on the sawdust pile beside the river and his old woman, what thoughts came into his mind? Could it be that, to Sponge, his old woman was like the river, like the sky overhead, like the trees on a distant river-shore? Was she to him like a fact in nature, something about which you asked no questions—something like birth or death?

Bruce decided the old man was not necessarily self-satisfied. With him being satisfied or not satisfied did not count. There was in him a kind of humbleness as in Tom Wills and he liked the skill of his own hands. That gave him something to rest on in life. Tom Wills would have liked the man. "He's got something on you and me," Tom would have said.

As to his old woman—he was used to her. Unlike many working-men's wives she did not look worn out. That might have been because she had never had but two children, but also it might have been because of something else. There was a thing worth doing her man could do better than most other men. He rested in that fact and his wife rested in him. The man and woman had stayed within the limits of their powers, had moved freely within a small but clear circle of life. The old woman cooked well and she liked going off with Sponge on an occasional spree—they dignified by calling it "going fishing." She was a tough wiry little thing and did not get tired of life—of Sponge her husband.

Being satisfied or not satisfied with life had nothing to do with Sponge Martin. On Saturday afternoon when he and Bruce were getting ready to leave he threw up his hands and declaimed: "Saturday night and supper on the table. It's the happiest time in a working-man's life." Was Bruce out for something very like Sponge had got? It might be he had left Bernice just because she did not know how to team with him. She hadn't wanted to team with him. What had she wanted? Well, never mind her. Bruce had been thinking of her all afternoon, of her and his mother, what he could remember of his mother.

Very likely a man like Sponge did not go around, as he did, with his brain churning—fancies drifting—a feeling of being all corked up—unreleased. It must be that most men got into a place, after a time, where all stood still. Little fragments of thoughts flying about in the mind. Nothing organized. The thoughts getting further and further away.

There was a log he had once, as a boy, seen bobbing on the face of the river. It got further and further away, was presently just a tiny black spot. Then it went, disappeared into the vast flowing grayness. It did not go suddenly. When you were gazing hard at it, trying to see just how long it could be kept in sight, then—

Was it there? It was! It wasn't! It was! It wasn't!

A trick of the mind. Suppose most men were dead and did not know it. When you were alive, a surge of thoughts, fancies, through the mind. Perhaps if you got the thoughts and fancies organized a little, made them work through your body, made thoughts and fancies a part of yourself—

They might be used then—perhaps as Sponge Martin used a brush. You might lay them on something as Sponge Martin could lay varnish on. Suppose about one man in a million got things organized a little. What would that mean? What would such a man be?

Would he be a Napoleon, a Cæsar?

Not likely. That would be too much bother. If he became a Napoleon or a Cæsar he would have to be thinking all the time of the others, trying to use the others, trying to wake them up. Well, no, he wouldn't try to wake them up. If they woke up they would be just like him. "I like not his lean and hungry look. He thinks too much." That sort of thing, eh? A Napoleon or a Cæsar would have to give others toys to play with, an army—conquests. He would have to make a display before them, have wealth, wear fine clothes, make them all envious, make them all want to be as he was.

Bruce had many thoughts about Sponge as he worked beside him in the shop, as he walked beside him along a street, as he saw him sleeping on the floor like a pig or a dog, after stuffing himself with food his old woman had cooked. Sponge had lost his carriage-painting shop through no fault of his own. There were too few carriages to paint. Later he might have set up a shop to paint automobiles if he had wanted to, but it was likely he was getting too old for that. He would keep on painting wheels, talking of the time when he did own a shop, eating, sleeping, getting drunk. When he and his old woman were a little drunk she seemed like a kid to him and he became like a kid, for a time. How often? About four times a week, Sponge said once, laughing. He might have been bragging. Bruce tried to imagine himself Sponge at such a moment, Sponge lying on the sawdust pile beside the river with his old woman. He couldn't do it. What got mixed up in such fancies was his own reaction to life. He couldn't be Sponge, the old workman robbed of his position as a master workman—drunk and trying to be like a kid with an old woman. What happened was that at the thought certain unpleasant experiences of his own life came up to mock him. Once he had read a book by Zola, "La Terre," and later, but a short time before he left Chicago, Tom Wills had shown him a new book by the Irishman Joyce, "Ulysses." There were certain pages. A man named Bloom standing on a beach near some women. A woman, Bloom's wife, in her bedroom at home. The thoughts of the woman—her night of animalism—all set down—minutely. Realism in writing lifted up sharp to something burning and raw like a raw sore. Others coming to look at the sores. For Bruce, to try to think of Sponge and his wife in their hour of pleasure in each other, such pleasure as youth knew, was like that. It left a faint unpleasant smell in his nostrils—like decayed eggs—dumped in a wood—across the river—far off.

Oh, Lord! Was his own mother—on the boat, that time they saw the crazy man and the young fellow with the mustache—was she, at that moment, a kind of Bloom?

Bruce did not want that thought. The figure of Bloom had seemed true to him, beautifully true, but it had sprung out of a brain not his. A European, a Continental man—that Joyce. Over there men had lived in one place a long time and had deposited something of themselves everywhere. A sensitive man walking there, living there, got it into his being. In America much of the land was still new, unsoiled. Hang on to the sun, the wind and the rain.

A LAME ONE
TO J. J.

At night when there are no lights, my city is a man who arises from a bed to stare into darkness.

In the daytime my city is the son of a dreamer. He has become the companion of thieves and prostitutes. He has denied his father.

My city is a thin little old man who lives in a rooming-house in a dirty street. He wears false teeth that have become loose and make a sharp clicking sound when he eats. He cannot find himself a woman and indulges in self-abuse. He picks cigar-ends out of the gutter.

My city lives in the roofs of the houses, in the eaves. A woman came to my city and he threw her far down, out of the eaves onto a pile of stones. Those who live in my city declare she fell.

There is an angry man whose wife is unfaithful. He is my city. My city is in his hair, in his breath, in his eyes. When he breathes his breath is the breath of my city.

There are many cities standing in rows. There are cities that sleep, cities that stand in the mud of swamps.

My city is very strange. It is tired and nervous. My city has become a woman whose lover is ill. She creeps in the hallways of a house and listens at the door of a room.

I cannot tell what my city is like.

My city is a kiss from the feverish lips of many tired people.

My city is a murmur of voices coming out of a pit.

Had Bruce fled from his own city, Chicago, hoping to find, in the soft nights of a river town, something to cure him?

What was he up to? Suppose it was something like this—suppose that young man in the boat had suddenly said to the woman sitting there with the child, "I know you aren't going to live very long and that you will not have any more children. I know everything about you that you, yourself, cannot know." There might be such a thing as moments when men and men, women and women, men and women could get like that toward each other. "Ships that pass in the night." It was the sort of thing it made a man seem silly to himself to think about definitely but it was quite sure there was something that people like himself, his mother before him, that young man on the river packet, people scattered about, here and there, that they were after.

Bruce's mind flopped back. Since he had left Bernice he had done a lot of thinking and feeling he had never done before and that was something gained. He might not be getting anywhere in particular but he was having fun of a sort and he wasn't bored as he had formerly been. The hours in the shop varnishing wheels did not cut much figure. You could varnish wheels and think of anything you pleased and the more skillful your hands became the more freedom your mind and your fancy had. There was a kind of pleasure in the passing hours. Sponge, the unmalicious, the man child, playing, bragging, talking, showing Bruce how to varnish wheels accurately and well. It was the first time in his life Bruce had ever done anything well with his hands.

If a man got so he could use his own thoughts, his own feelings, his own fancies as Sponge could use a paint-brush, what then? What would the man be like?

Would that be what an artist was? It would be a fine to-do, if he, Bruce, in running away from Bernice and her crowd, from the conscious artists, had only done so because he wanted to be just what they wanted to be. Men and women in Bernice's crowd were always talking of being artists, speaking of themselves as artists. Why had men, like Tom Wills and himself, a kind of contempt for them? Did he and Tom Wills secretly want to be artists of another sort? Was that what he, Bruce, had been up to when he lit out from Bernice and when he came back to Old Harbor? Was there something in the town he had missed as a boy there—he wanted to find—some string he wanted to pick up?

CHAPTER FOURTEEN

SATURDAY evening and Bruce walking out at the shop door with Sponge. The other workman, the surly man at the next bench, had gone hurriedly out just ahead of them, had hurried out without saying good-night and Sponge had winked at Bruce.

"He wants to get home quick to see if his old woman is still there—wants to see if she has gone off with that other chap she is always fooling with. He comes to her house in the afternoon. No danger his wanting to take her. He'd have to support her then. She'd go fast enough if he asked her but he won't. Much better let this one do the work and make the money to feed and clothe her, eh?"

Why had Bruce called Sponge unmalicious? Lord knows he was malicious enough. There was a thing called manhood, maleness, he had, and that he was proud of—as he was of his craftsmanship. He had got his own woman fast and hard and had contempt for any man who couldn't do the same thing. His contempt had no doubt leaked across to the workman beside him and had made him more surly than he would have been had Sponge treated him as he did Bruce.

When he came into the shop in the morning Bruce always spoke to the man at the second wheel-peg and he thought the man sometimes looked at him wistfully, as though to say, "If I could get a chance to tell you, if I knew how to tell you there would be my side to the story, too. I'm what I am. If I lost one woman I wouldn't ever know how to go at it to get me another. I ain't the kind that get 'em easy. I ain't got the nerve. To tell the truth, and if you only knew it, I'm a good deal more like you than this Sponge. With him everything is down in his hands. He gets everything out of him through his hands. Take his woman away and he would get another with his hands. I'm like you. I'm a thinker, a dreamer maybe. I'm the kind that makes a mess of his life."

How much easier for Bruce to be, in fancy, the surly silent workman than for him to be Sponge. Still it was Sponge he liked, wanted to be like. Did he? Anyway he wanted to be, partly, like him.

In the street outside the factory as the two men walked across railroad tracks and up along a climbing cobblestone street toward the business part of Old Harbor, in the gathering dusk of the early spring evening, Sponge was smiling. It was the same kind of detached, half-malicious smile Bruce used to wear sometimes in Bernice's presence and that always drove her half mad. It wasn't directed at Bruce. Sponge was thinking of the surly workman, strutting like a rooster because he was more the man—more male. Had Bruce been up to some such trick with Bernice? No doubt he had. Lordy, she ought to be glad he wasn't around any more.

His thoughts whirling on. His thoughts centered

on the surly workman now. Awhile before, but a few minutes before, he had tried to imagine himself Sponge lying on a sawdust pile under the stars, Sponge with his hide full of whisky, and his old woman lying beside him. He had tried to fancy himself, under such circumstances, the stars shining down, the river running silently near at hand, had tried to imagine himself under such circumstances, feeling like a kid and feeling the woman beside him as a kid. It hadn't worked. What he would do, what such a fellow as himself would do under such circumstances he knew only too well. He would awake in the cold morning light, having thoughts, too many thoughts. What he had succeeded in doing was to make himself feel, at the moment, very ineffectual. He had re-created himself, in the fancy of the moment, not as Sponge, the effectual, the direct, the man who could give himself completely, but himself in some of his own more ineffectual moments. He had remembered times, two or three of them, when he had been with women and had been ineffectual. Perhaps he had been ineffectual with Bernice. Had he been ineffectual or had she?

Much easier after all to imagine himself the surly workman. That he could really do. He could imagine himself beaten by a woman, afraid of her. He could imagine himself a fellow like that Bloom in the book "Ulysses" and it was evident that Joyce, the writer and dreamer, was in the same boat. He had certainly done his Bloom much better than he had his Stephen, had made him a lot more real—and Bruce, in fancy, could make the surly workman more real than

Sponge, could enter into him more quickly, understand him better. He could be the surly ineffectual workman, could, in fancy, be the man in bed with the wife —could lie there afraid, angry, hopeful, full of pretense. That is what he had been with Bernice perhaps —partly, anyway. Why hadn't he told her, when she was writing that story, why hadn't he told her with an oath what rot it was, what it really meant? Instead he had worn that grin that had so puzzled and angered her. He had fled into the recesses of his own mind where she could not follow and from that vantage-point had grinned out at her.

Now he was walking up along a street with Sponge and Sponge was grinning the same kind of a grin he himself had so often worn in Bernice's presence. They had been sitting together, dining perhaps, and she had suddenly got up from a table and had said: "I've got to go write now." Then the grin had come. Often it knocked her off her pins for a whole day. She couldn't write a word. What a dirty trick, really!

Sponge, however, was doing it, not to him, Bruce, but to the surly workman. Bruce was reasonably sure of that. He felt safe.

They had got to the town's business street and were walking along with crowds of other workmen, all employees of the wheel factory. A car carrying young Grey, the owner of the factory, and his wife, climbed up the hill on second speed, the engine making a sharp whining sound, and passed near them. The woman at the wheel turned to look. It was Sponge told Bruce who was in the car.

"She's been coming down there quite often lately. She totes him home. She's one he got away from here somewhere, when he was in the war. I don't think he's really got her. Maybe she's lonesome, in a strange town where there ain't many of her kind, and likes to come down to the factory at quitting-time to look 'em over. She's been looking you over pretty regularly lately. I've noticed it."

Sponge was smiling. Well, it wasn't a smile. It was a grin. At the moment Bruce thought he looked like a wise old Chinaman—something of that sort. He became self-conscious. Sponge might be making fun of him as he did of the surly workman at the next bench. In the picture Bruce had made of his fellow workman, and that he liked, Sponge surely did not have many very subtle thoughts. It would have been something of a come-down for Bruce to think of the workman as very sensitive to impressions. There was no doubt he had got rather a jump out of the woman in the car and it had happened three times now. To think of Sponge as being very sensitive would be like thinking of Bernice as better than he would ever be at the very thing he wanted most to be. Bruce wanted to be preeminent in something—in being more sensitive to everything going on about him than others could possibly be.

They came to the corner where Bruce turned upward to go toward his hotel, Sponge still wearing that smile. He kept urging Bruce to come to his house to dinner on Sunday. "All right," Bruce said, "and I'll manage to get a bottle. There's a young doc living at the hotel. I'll tackle him for a prescription. I guess he'll come across all right."

Sponge kept smiling, having a good time with his own thoughts. "It would be a jolt. You ain't exactly like the rest of us. Maybe you make her think of someone she's been stuck on before. I wouldn't so much mind seeing a Grey get a jolt like that."

As though not wanting Bruce to comment on what he had said the old workman changed the subject quickly. "There's something I been wanting to tell you. You better look a little out. Sometimes you get a look on your face exactly like that Smedley," he said, laughing. Smedley was the surly workman.

Still smiling Sponge walked away along the street, Bruce standing to watch him go. As though conscious of being watched he strutted a little, straightening his old shoulders as though to say—"He don't think I know as much as I do." The sight made Bruce also grin.

"I guess I know what he means but there's small chance of that. I didn't leave Bernice, looking for some other woman. I've got another bee in my bonnet although I don't just know what it is," he thought as he climbed the hill toward the hotel. Thinking that Sponge had shot and missed he felt relieved and rather happy. "It wouldn't do to have the little cuss know more about me than I have been able to find out myself," he thought again.

BOOK SIX

BOOK SIX

CHAPTER FIFTEEN

PERHAPS she had figured it all out from the beginning and didn't quite dare tell herself. She saw him first, walking with a small man, heavily mustached, up a cobblestone street that led from her husband's factory, and the impression she had of her own feelings was just that she would like to stop him some evening as he came out at the factory door. It was the same feeling she had about that man in Paris, the one she saw at Rose Frank's apartment, and he had eluded her. She had never succeeded in getting near him, in hearing a word from his lips. Perhaps he had belonged to Rose and Rose had managed to keep him out of the way. Still Rose didn't seem that sort. She had seemed like one woman who would take a chance. It might be that this man and the one in Paris were alike unconscious of her. Aline did not want to do anything crude. She thought of herself as a lady. And then, too, there was nothing in life at all if you could not get at things in some subtle way. Plenty of women went after men openly—drove straight at them —but what did they get? No use getting a man as a man and in no other way. She had Fred, her husband, that way—had, she thought, all he had to offer.

It wasn't so much—a kind of sweet childlike faith in her, hardly justified, she thought. He had a fixed notion of what a woman, the wife of a man in his position, should be and he took it for granted she was what he thought. Fred took too much for granted.

Outwardly she was all he expected. That was hardly the point. One couldn't prevent oneself having thoughts. There might be nothing to life but just that —living—seeing the days pass—being a wife and perhaps presently a mother — dreaming — keeping the thing, down inside, in order. If one couldn't always keep it in order at least one could keep it out of sight. You walked in a certain way—wore the right clothes —knew how to talk—kept up a kind of touch with the arts, with music, painting, the new moods in house furnishings—read the latest novels. You and your husband had together a certain position to maintain and you did your share. He looked to you for certain things, the keeping-up of a certain style—appearances. In a town like Old Harbor, Indiana, it wasn't so hard.

And anyway a man who worked in a factory was likely to be a factory-hand — nothing more. You couldn't be thinking of him. His resemblance to that other man she had seen in Rose's apartment was no doubt a physical accident. There was about the two men the same air, a kind of readiness to give and not ask much. One thought of such a man going along, quite casually, becoming absorbed in something, burning himself out in it, then dropping it—as casually perhaps. Burning himself out in what? Well, say in some kind of work, or in the love of a woman. Did she want to be loved like that, by that sort of a man?

"Well, I do! Every woman does. We don't get it

though, and if it were offered, most of us would be afraid. We are pretty practical and hard-headed, at bottom, all of us, we're made that way. It's what a woman is, that sort of thing.

"I wonder why we are always trying to create the other illusion, feeding on it ourselves?"

One has to think. The days pass. They are too much alike—the days. An imagined experience is not the same as one actually gone through, but it is something. When a woman has been married things change for her. She has to try to keep up the illusion that everything is as it was before. It can't be, of course. We know too much.

Aline used to go for Fred quite often in the evening and when he was a little delayed the men came pouring out at the factory door and passed her as she sat at the wheel of the car. What did she mean to them? What did they mean to her? Dark figures in overalls, tall men, short men, old men, young men. She had got the one man quite fixed in her mind. That was Bruce as he came from the shop with Sponge Martin, the little old man with the black mustache. She did not know who Sponge was, had never heard of him, but he talked and the man beside him listened. Did he listen? At any rate he had only looked at her once or twice—a fleeting self-conscious glance.

How many men in the world! She had got herself a man who had money and position. That had been a lucky chance, maybe. She wasn't very young any more when Fred asked her to marry him, and sometimes she wondered dimly if she would have consented if marriage with him hadn't seemed such a perfect solution. You had to take chances in life and it was a good chance. By such a marriage you got a house, position, clothes, an automobile. If you were stuck off in a little Indiana town, eleven months out of the year, at least you were on top of the heap in the town. Cæsar riding through a miserable little town, going to join his army, Cæsar addressing a comrade, "Better be king on a dung-heap than a beggar in Rome." Something of that sort. Aline wasn't very accurate about quotations and it is sure she did not think the word "dung-heap." It wasn't the kind of word such women as herself knew anything about—wasn't in their vocabularies.

She thought about men a good deal, wondered about them. In Fred's notion of things everything was settled for her, but was it? When things got settled you were through, might as well sit rocking in a chair waiting for death. Death, before life came.

Aline hadn't any children yet. She wondered why. Hadn't Fred touched her deeply enough? Was there something in her still to be aroused, awakened from sleep?

Her thoughts drifted into a new channel and she became what she herself would have called cynical. It was, after all, rather amusing how she managed to impress people in Fred's town, how she managed to impress him. It might be that was because she had lived in Chicago and in New York and had been to Paris, because her husband Fred had become, since his father's death, the chief man of the town, because she had a knack for dress and a certain air.

When the women of the town came to call on her, the Judge's wife, the wife of Striker, the cashier of the bank in which Fred was by far the largest stock-holder—the doctor's wife—when they came to her house they thought it up to them to talk of cultural things, of books, music and painting. Everyone knew she had been an art student. That confused and both-ered them. It was quite sure she wasn't a favorite in the town but the women did not dare pay her out for snubbing them a little. If one of them could get some-thing on her they might make mince-meat of her, but how were they to do anything of that sort? Even to think of such a thing was a little vulgar. Aline did not like such thoughts.

There was nothing to be got on her, never would be.

Aline at the wheel of an expensive automobile watched Bruce Dudley and Sponge Martin going up a cobblestone street among many other working-men. They were the only two of all the men she had seen come out at the factory door who seemed much inter-ested in each other, and what an odd-looking pair they were. The younger man did not look much like a laborer. Well, what did a laborer look like? What differentiated a laborer from another man, from the kind of men who were Fred's friends, from the kind of men she had known at her father's house in Chicago when she was a young girl? One might fancy that a laborer would naturally look humble, but it was certain that the little broad-backed man had nothing humble about him, and as for Fred, her own husband, there had been when she first saw him nothing to mark him as anything special. Perhaps she was only attracted to the two men because they seemed interested in each other. The little old man was so cocky. He went along up the cobblestone street like a banty rooster. If Aline had been more like Rose Frank and that crowd of hers in Paris she would have thought of Sponge Martin as a man always liking to strut before women as a rooster struts before hens, and such a thought, put in somewhat different terms, did in fact cross her mind. Smiling, she thought that Sponge might very well have been a Napoleon Bonaparte walking along like that, stroking a black mustache with stubby fingers. The mustache was a bit too black for such an old man. It was shiny—coal-black. Perhaps he dyed it, the cocky little old thing. One had to get amusement somehow, had to think about something.

What was keeping Fred? Since his father had died and he had come into his money Fred certainly took life pretty seriously. He seemed to feel the weight of things on his shoulders, was always talking as though everything would go to pieces at the factory if he did not stay on the job all the time. She wondered how much of his talk about the importance of the things he did was true?

CHAPTER SIXTEEN

ALINE had met her husband Fred at Rose Frank's apartment in Paris. That was during the summer after the so-called World War came to an end and it was an evening to be remembered. Funny, too, about this World business. The Anglo-Saxons, the Nordics, were always using the word—best in the world—biggest in the world, world wars, champions of the world.

You go along in life, not thinking very much, not feeling very much, not knowing very much—about yourself or anyone else—thinking life is so and so, and then—bang! Something happens. You aren't at all what you had thought you were. A lot of people found that out during the war.

Under certain circumstances you had thought you knew just about what you would do, but all of your thoughts were, as likely as not, lies. After all, it might be, you never knew anything really until it had touched your own life, your own body. There is a tree growing in a field. Is it really a tree? What is a tree? Go touch it with your fingers. Stand back several feet and hurl your body against it. It is unyielding—like a rock. How rough the bark is! Your shoulder hurts. There is blood on your cheek.

A tree is something to you but what is it to another?

Suppose it were your job to cut the tree down. You lay an ax to its body, to its sturdy trunk. Some trees bleed when injured, others weep bitter tears. Once when Aline Aldridge was a child, her father—who had an interest in turpentine forests somewhere in the South—came home from a trip down there and was talking with another man in the living-room of the Aldridge house. He told how they cut and maimed the trees to get the sap for the turpentine. Aline had been sitting in the room, on a stool by her father's knee, and had heard it all—the story of a vast forest of trees all cut and maimed. For what? To get turpentine. What was turpentine? Was it some strange golden elixir of life?

What a tale! When it was told, Aline grew a little pale, but her father and his friend did not notice. Her father had been giving a technical description of the process of producing turpentine. The men were not thinking her thoughts, did not sense her thoughts. Later in her bed that night she cried. What did they want to do it for? Why did they want their blamed old turpentine?

Trees crying out—bleeding. Men going about, hurting them, cutting them with axes. Some of the trees fell down groaning, while others stood up, the blood running from them, crying out to the child in the bed. The trees had eyes, they had arms, legs and bodies. A forest of injured trees, staggering about, bleeding. The ground under the trees was red with blood.

When the World War came on and Aline had become

a woman she remembered her father's story of the turpentine-trees, how they got their turpentine. Her brother George, three years older than herself, was killed in France, and Teddy Copeland, the young man she was engaged to marry, died of the "flu" in an American camp; and in her consciousness of them they did not remain as dead men, but as men injured and bleeding, far off, in some strange place. Neither the brother nor Ted Copeland had seemed very near to her, no nearer perhaps than the trees of the forest of the story. She had not touched them closely. She had said she would marry Copeland because he was going off to war and had asked her. It had seemed the right thing to do. Could you say "no" to a young man at such a time—going off to be killed perhaps? It would have seemed like saying "no" to one of the trees. Suppose you were asked to bind up one of the trees' wounds and said "no." Well, Teddy Copeland had not been exactly a tree. He had been a young man and a very handsome one. Had she married him Aline's father and brother would have been pleased.

When the war was over Aline went for a visit to Paris with Esther Walker and her husband Joe, the painter who did the portrait of her dead brother from a photograph. He also did one of Teddy Copeland for his father and then another of Aline's dead mother —getting five thousand dollars for each—and Aline had been the one who had told her father about the painter. She had seen a portrait of his at the Art Institute, where she then was a student, and had told her father of him. Then she met Esther Walker and invited her and her husband out to the Aldridge house. Esther and Joe had both been good enough to say some very nice things about her own work, but that, she felt, was just politeness. Although she had a knack for drawing she hadn't taken her own cleverness very seriously. There was something about painting, real painting, she could not get at, could not understand. After the war started and her brother and Teddy went away she wanted to do something and could not bring herself to the business of working every minute to "help win the war" by knitting socks or running about selling Liberty Bonds. The war in fact bored her. She did not know what it was about. If it had not come on she would have married Ted Copeland and then—then at least she would have found out some things.

Young men going away to be killed, thousands of them, hundreds of thousands. How many women felt as she did? It was taking something away from women, the chances for something. Suppose you are a field and it is spring. A farmer is coming toward you with a bag filled with seed. Now he has almost reached the field, but instead of coming to plant the seed he stops by the roadside and burns it. Women can't have such thoughts, not directly. They can't if they are nice women.

Better to go in for art, take painting lessons—particularly if you are rather clever with a brush. If you can't do that go in for culture—read the latest books, go to the theater, go to hear music. When music is being played—certain kinds of music—— But never mind that. That also is something a nice woman doesn't talk about or think about.

There are a lot of things to be let alone in life—that's sure.

Until after she reached Paris, Aline did not know what kind of a painter Joe Walker was or what kind of a woman was Esther, but on the boat she began to suspect, and when she did get a hunch about them she had to smile to think how willing she had been to let Esther work things out for her. The painter's wife had been so quick and clever about paying Aline back. "You did a good turn for us—fifteen thousand is not to be sneezed at—now we'll do as much for you." There never had been, never would be, a thing so crude as a wink or a shrug of the shoulders from Esther. Aline's father had been deeply hurt by the tragedy of the war and his wife had been dead since Aline was a child of ten and while she was in Chicago and Joe was at work on the portraits—you can't do five-thousand-dollar portraits too fast, you must take at least two or three weeks for each—while she was practically living at the Aldridge house Esther made the older man feel almost as though he again had a wife to look after him.

She spoke with such reverence of the man's character and of the undoubted ability of the daughter. "Such men as you have made such sacrifices. It is the quiet man of ability going straight alone, helping to keep the social order intact, meeting every contingency without a murmur—it is such men who—it is a thing one can't speak of openly, but in times like this, when the whole social order has been shaken, when old standards of life are being torn down, when the young have lost faith——"

"We who are of an older order—we must be father and mother to the younger generation now."

"Beauty will persist—the things worth while in life will persist."

"Poor Aline—to have lost both a prospective husband and a brother. And she has such talent, too. She is like you, very quiet, not saying much. A year abroad now may save her from some kind of a breakdown."

How easily Esther had befuddled Aline's father, the shrewd and capable corporation lawyer. Men were really altogether too easy. There was no doubt Aline should have stayed at home—in Chicago. A man, any man unmarried, with money, should not be left lying about loose with such women as Esther about. Although she had not had much experience Aline was no fool. Esther knew that. When Joe Walker came to the Aldridge house in Chicago to paint the portraits Aline was twenty-six. When she sat at the wheel of her husband's car, that evening before the factory in Old Harbor, she was twenty-nine.

What a jumble! What a mixed unaccountable thing life could be!

CHAPTER SEVENTEEN

MARRIAGE! Had she intended marriage, had Fred really intended marriage that night in Paris when both Rose Frank and Fred rather went off their heads, one after the other? How did one ever happen to get married anyway? How did it come about? What did people think they were up to when they did it? What made a man, after he had known dozens of women, suddenly decide to marry a particular one?

Fred had been a young American in an Eastern college, an only son with a rich father, then a soldier, a rich man rather grandly enlisting as a common private —to help win a war—then in an American training camp—later in France. When the first American contingent went through England the English women— war-starved—the English women—

American women too, "Help win the war!"

What a lot Fred must have known he had never told Aline about.

. . . . .

On the evening as she sat in the car before the factory in Old Harbor, Fred surely was taking his time. He had told her there was an advertising man coming down from Chicago and he might decide to do a thing called "putting on a national advertising campaign."

The factory was making a lot of money and if a man didn't spend some of it to build up good-will for the future he would have to pay it all out in taxes. Advertising was an asset, a legitimate expenditure. Fred thought he would try advertising. It was likely he was in his office now talking to the advertising man from Chicago.

It was growing dark in the shadow of the factory, but why snap on the lights. It was nice to sit in half-darkness by the wheel, thinking. A slender woman in a rather elegant dress, a good hat—one she had got from Paris—long slender fingers resting on a driving-wheel, men in overalls passing out at a factory door and across a dusty road, passing very near the car—tall men —short men—a low murmur of men's voices.

A certain humbleness in working-men passing such a car, such a woman.

Very little humbleness in a short, broad-shouldered old man, stroking a too-black mustache with stubby fingers. He seemed to want to laugh at Aline. "I'm onto you," he seemed to want to shout—the cocky little old thing. His companion—to whom he seemed devoted—did look like that man in Rose's apartment in Paris—that night—that so important night.

That night in Paris, when Aline first saw Fred! She had gone with Esther and Joe Walker to Rose Frank's apartment because both Esther and Joe thought they had better. By that time Esther and Joe amused Aline. She had a notion that, had they stayed in America long enough and had her father seen more of them, he also would have caught on—after a time.

After all, they had rather had him at a disadvantage—talking of art and beauty—that sort of thing to a man who had just lost a son in the war, a son whose portrait Joe was painting—and getting a very good likeness.

Never such a couple for looking out for the main chance—never such a couple for educating a rather quick shrewd woman like Aline. Little enough danger such a couple ever staying in one spot too long. Their arrangement with Aline had been something quite special. No words about it. No words necessary. "We'll give you a peep under the tent at the show and you take no chances. We're married. We're quite respectable—always know the best people, you can see for yourself. That's the advantage of being our kind of artists. You see all sides of life and take no chance. New York is getting more and more like Paris every year. But Chicago . . ."

Aline had lived in New York two or three times, for some months each time, with her father, when he had important business there. They had lived at an expensive hotel, but it was evident the Walkers knew things about modern New York life Aline did not know.

They had succeeded in making Aline's father feel comfortable about her—and perhaps he felt comfortable with her away—for a time at least. Esther had been able to convey that notion to Aline. It had been a good arrangement for all concerned.

And certainly, she thought, educational to Aline. Such people, really! How odd that her father, a clever man in his own way, hadn't caught onto them quicker.

They worked like a team, getting men like her father at five thousand each. Solid respectable people, Joe and Esther. Esther worked that string hard, and Joe, who never ran any risks by being seen in any but the best company—when they were in America—who painted very skillfully and who talked just boldly enough but not too boldly—he also helped to make thick and warm the art atmosphere when they were getting a new prospect lined up.

Aline smiled in the darkness. What a sweet little cynic I am. You could live over, in fancy, a whole year of your life while you waited, perhaps three minutes, for your husband to come out at a factory door and then you could run up a hillside and overtake two workmen, the sight of whom had started your brain working, could overtake them before they had walked three blocks up a hillside street.

As for Esther Walker, Aline thought she had got on rather well with her that summer in Paris. When they had got off for Europe together both women had been ready enough to put the cards on the table. Aline had made a great pretense of being deeply interested in art —perhaps it wasn't all just pretense—and had that talent of hers for making little drawings, and Esther had done a lot of talking about hidden ability that should be brought out, all that sort of thing.

"You are onto me and I am onto you. Let's ride along together, saying nothing about the matter." Saying nothing Esther had managed to convey about that message to the young woman and Aline had fallen in with her mood. Well, it wasn't a mood. Such people didn't have moods. What they did was to play a game. If you wanted to play with them they could be very friendly and sweet.

Aline had got it all, a confirmation of about what she had thought, one night on the boat, and had to think fast and hold onto herself hard—for perhaps thirty seconds—while she made up her own mind about something. What an ugly lonely feeling! She had to hold her fists doubled and there was a fight to prevent tears coming.

Then she fell for it—decided to play the game out—with Esther. Joe didn't count. You get educated fast if you only let yourself. She can't touch me, inside, maybe. I'll ride along and keep my eyes open.

She had. They were rotten really, the Walkers, but Esther had something in her. She was outwardly the hard one, the schemer, but inside there was something she tried to hold onto and that had never been touched. It was sure her husband, Joe Walker, could never touch it and Esther was perhaps too cautious to take chances with another man. Once later she gave Aline a hint. "The man was young and I had just married Joe. It was during the year before the war started. For about an hour I thought I would and then I didn't. It would have given Joe an advantage I didn't dare let him have. I'm not one who would ever go the whole road—ruin myself. The young chap was the reckless sort—a young American boy. I decided I had better not. You understand."

She had tried something on Aline—that time on the boat. What was it Esther had tried? One night when

Joe was talking with several people, telling them about modern painting, telling them about Cézanne and Picasso and the others, talking suavely, kindly, about the rebels in the arts, Esther and Aline went off to sit in chairs on another part of the deck. Two young men came along and tried to join them, but Esther knew how to fence off without giving offense. She evidently thought Aline knew more than she did, but it was not Aline's part to attempt to disillusion her.

What an instinct, away down inside, to preserve something!

What was it Esther had tried on Aline?

There are a lot of things you can't get down in words, even in your own thoughts. What Esther had talked about was a love that asked nothing, and how really beautiful that sounded! "It should be between two people of the same sex. Between yourself and a man it won't work. I've tried it," she said.

She had taken Aline's hand and for a long time they sat in silence, an odd creepy feeling deep down in Aline. What a test—to play the game out with such a woman —not to let her know what your instincts are doing to you—down inside—not to let the hands tremble—to make no physical sign of any shrinking. The woman's soft voice, with the caress in it, a kind of sincerity too. "They get each other in a more subtle way. It lasts longer. It takes longer to understand but it lasts longer. There is something white and fine you try for. I've waited a long time for just you, maybe. As far as Joe is concerned I have been all right with him. It's a little hard to talk. There's so much that can't be said. In Chicago, when I saw you out there, I thought, 'At your age most women in your position have married.' You'll have to do that sometime too, I suppose, but it makes a difference to me that you haven't yet— that you hadn't when I found you. It's getting so if a man and another man or two women are seen too much together there is talk. America is getting almost as sophisticated, as wise, as Europe. That's where husbands are a big help. You help them all you can, whatever their game is, but you keep all the best of yourself for the other—for the one who understands what you are really driving at."

Aline moved restlessly at the wheel of the car thinking of that evening on the boat and all it had meant. Had it been the beginning of sophistication for her? Life isn't just as it is set down in the copy-books. How much dare you let yourself find out? A game of life— a game of death. Very easy to let yourself become romantic—and scared. American women surely have had things easy. Their men know so little—dare let themselves know so little. You can keep out of deciding anything if you wish, but is it any fun, never to be in the know—on the inside? If you look into life, know much of the taint of life, can you keep outside yourself? "Not much," Aline's father would no doubt have said, and it was something of that sort her husband Fred would have said too. You have to live your own life then. When her boat left the shores of America it left behind more than Aline wanted to think about. President Wilson had been finding out something of the sort at about that time. It killed him.

At any rate it was sure that the talk with Esther had made Aline the more ready to marry Fred Grey when she came to him later. Besides, it had made her less exacting, less sure of herself, the others, most of the others she had seen that summer in the company of Joe and Esther. Fred had been, he was, as fine as, say, a well-bred dog. If what he had was American she was glad enough, as a woman, to take American chances— she thought at the time.

Esther's talk had been so slow and soft. Aline could think of it all, remember it all very clearly in a few seconds, but it must have taken Esther longer to say all the sentences needed to convey her meaning.

And the meaning Aline had to jump at, knowing nothing, get instinctively or not at all. Esther would be one to leave herself always a clear alibi. She was a very clever woman, no doubt of that. Joe had been lucky to get her, being what he was.

It hadn't worked, not yet.

You come up and you go down. A woman of twenty-six, if she have anything in her at all, is ready. And if she hasn't anything in her, another one, like Esther, doesn't want her at all. If you want a fool, a romantic fool, what about a man, a good American business man? He'll do well enough and you remain safe and sound. Nothing ever really touches you at all. A long life lived and you always high and dry and safe. Do you want that?

It was really as though Aline had been pushed by Esther off the side of the steamboat into the sea. And the sea was very lovely that evening when Esther talked to her. That may have been one reason why Aline kept feeling safe. You get something outside you that way, like the sea, and it helps just because it is lovely. There is the sea, little waves breaking, the sea running white behind the ship's wake, washing against the side of the ship like soft silk tearing, and in the sky stars coming out slowly. Why is it that when you twist things out of their natural order, when you become a little sophisticated and want more than you ever did before, the risk is relatively greater? So easy to become rotten. A tree never gets that way because it is a tree.

A voice talking, a hand touching your arm in just a certain way. Words coming far apart. Over on the other side the boat, Joe, Esther's husband, talking that stuff of art. Several ladies gathered about Joe. Afterwards they would speak of it, quoting his words. "As my friend Joseph Walker, the famous portrait-painter, you know, said to me—Cézanne is so and so. Picasso is so and so."

Take it that you are an American woman of twenty-six, trained as the daughter of a well-to-do Chicago lawyer would be trained, unsophisticated but shrewd, your body fresh and strong. You have had a dream. Well, young Copeland you had thought you were about to marry, was not quite the dream. He was nice enough. Not quite in the know enough—in some odd way. Most American men never get to be beyond seventeen—perhaps.

Take it you were that way and had been pushed off a boat into the sea. Joe's wife Esther has done that little thing for you. What would you do? Try to save yourself? Down you go—down and down, cutting through the surface of the sea fast enough. Oh, Lord, there are a lot of spots in life the mind of the average man and woman never touches at all. I wonder why not? Everything—at least most things—are obvious enough. Perhaps even a tree is not a tree for you until you have banged against it. Why is the lid lifted for some, while everything remains sound and water-tight for others? Those women on the deck listening to Joe as he talks—gabblers. Joe with his artist-merchant's eye peeled. Like as not either he or Esther put down names and addresses in a little book. Good idea their going across every summer. Back in the fall. People like to meet artists and writers on a boat. It's a touch of what Europe stands for, right near, at first hand. Lots of them work it. And don't the Americans fall for it! Fish come to the bait! Both Esther and Joe having moments of dreadful weariness just the same.

What you do when you are pushed off like that, as Aline was by Esther, is to hold your breath and not get rattled or indignant. There isn't anything to it if you go getting indignant. If you think Esther can't make a getaway, can't clear her own skirts, you don't know much.

After you cut through the surface you think only of coming up again as clear and clean as when you went down. Down below all is cold and wet—death, that road. You know the poets. Come and die with me. Our hands clasped together in death. The white long road together. Man and man, woman and woman. That sort of love—with Esther. What is life about? Who cares about life going on—in new forms, created out of ourselves?

If you're one sort, it's white dead fish to you—nothing else. You have to figure it out for yourself, and if you're the kind no one pushes off the boat, the whole thing will never come your way and you're safe. Maybe you're hardly interesting enough ever to be in danger. Most people walk high and safe—all their days.

.   .   .   .   .

Americans, eh? You got something out of it anyway, going to Europe with a woman like Esther. After that one time Esther never tried again. She had it all figured out. If Aline wasn't to be something she wanted for herself she could use her anyway. The Aldridge family stood well in Chicago and there would be other portraits to do out there. Esther had learned, fast enough, how people in general felt about art. If Aldridge Senior had Joe Walker do two portraits and they looked to him when finished as he thought his wife and his son had looked, then he would be likely to boost the Walker game in Chicago, and having paid five thousand each he would value the portraits the more for just that reason. "The greatest painter living, I think," Esther could imagine his saying to his Chicago friends.

The daughter Aline might get wiser but she wouldn't be likely to talk. When Esther had her mind made up about Aline she covered up her trail very neatly—did it well enough that evening on the boat and made her position stronger on that other evening, after six weeks in Paris, when she, Aline and Joe walked together over to Rose Frank's apartment. On that particular evening, when Aline had seen something of the Walkers' life in Paris and when Esther thought her a good deal more in the know, she kept talking to Aline in low tones, and Joe walked along without hearing, without trying to hear. The evening was very lovely and they walked along the left bank of the Seine, turning away from the river at the Chambre des Députés. People were sitting in little cafés on the rue Voltaire and over the scene hung the clear Parisian evening light—the painter's light. "Over here you've got to look out for both women and men," Esther said. "We Americans are considered fools by most Europeans just because there are things we don't want to know. It's because we are from a new country and have a kind of freshness and health in us."

Esther had said a lot of things of that sort to Aline. What she was really saying was something quite different. She was really denying that she had meant anything that night on the boat. "If you think I did, it is because you aren't very nice yourself." Something of that sort she was saying. Aline let it fly over her head. That night on the boat she had won the battle, she thought. There had been just a moment when she had to fight to get fresh air into her lungs, not to let her hands tremble as Esther held them, not to feel too utterly lonely and sad—leaving childhood—girlhood—

behind, like that, but after the one moment she was very quiet and mouselike, so much so that she had Esther a bit afraid of her—and that was really what she was after. It is always best to let the enemy clear away the dead after a battle—no fuss about that.

CHAPTER EIGHTEEN

FRED had come out at the factory door and was a little annoyed at Aline—or pretended to be—because she had been sitting in the car in the half-darkness without letting him know. The advertising man with whom he had been talking inside walked away up the street and Fred did not offer to give him a lift. That was because Aline was there. Fred would have had to introduce him. It would have made a new contact for both Fred and Aline, would have slightly changed the relationship between Fred and the man. Fred offered to drive but Aline laughed at him. She liked the feel of the car, a rather powerful one, as it ground its way up the steep streets. Fred lighted a cigar and before dropping away into his own thoughts made another protest about her sitting in the car in the gathering darkness and waiting there without letting him know. In reality he liked it, liked the notion of Aline, the wife, half servant, waiting for him, the man of affairs. "If I had wanted you I had but to blow the horn. As a matter of fact I could see you talking in there with that man through the window," Aline said.

The car ground its way up the street on second speed, and there was that man, standing at a corner under a light and still talking to the short broad-shouldered man. Surely he had a face very like that other man, the American she had seen at Rose Frank's apartment on the very evening she had met Fred. Odd that he should be a working-man in her husband's factory, and yet she remembered, that evening in Paris—the American in Rose's apartment had said to someone that he was once a working-man in an American factory. That was during a lull in the conversation and before Rose Frank's outbreak came. But why was this one so absorbed in the small man he was with? They weren't much alike—the two men.

Working-men, men coming out at the door of a factory, her husband's factory. Tall men, short men, broad men, slender men, lame men, men blind in one eye, a one-handed man, men in sweaty clothes. They went along, shuffle, shuffle—on the cobblestones in the roadway before a factory door, crossed railroad tracks, disappeared into a town. Her own house was at the top of a hill above the town, looking down on the town, looking down on the Ohio River where it made a great bend about the town, looking down on miles of low country where the valley of the river broadened out above and below town. In the winter all was gray in the valley. The river spreading out over the lowlands, becoming a vast gray sea. When he was a banker, Fred's father—"Old Grey" he was called by everyone in the town—had managed to get his hands on a lot of the valley land. In the early days they did not know how to work it profitably and because they couldn't build farm-houses and barns down there they thought the land was no good. As a matter of fact it was the richest land in the state. Every year the river overflowing left a fine gray silt on the land and that was marvelously enriching. The first farmers had tried to build levees, but when they broke, houses and barns were swept away in the floods.

Old Grey had waited like a spider. Farmers came to the bank and borrowed a little money on the cheap land and then let it go, let him foreclose. Had he been wise or had it all been an accident? Later it was found that, if you just let the water flow in and cover the land, it would run off again in the spring and leave that fine rich silt that made the corn grow almost like trees. What you did was to move out onto the land in the late spring with an army of hired men who lived in tents and in shacks set high up on stilts. You plowed and planted and the corn grew rank. Then you picked the corn and stored it in cribs, also built high up on stilts, and when the floods came again you sent barges out over the flooded lands to bring in the corn. You made money hand over fist. Fred had told Aline all about it. Fred thought that his father had been one of the shrewdest men that ever lived. He spoke of him, sometimes, as the Bible spoke of Father Abraham. "The Nestor of the house of Grey," something of that sort. What did Fred think about the fact that his wife had brought him no children? No doubt he had many queer thoughts about her when he was alone. That was why he sometimes acted so half frightened when she looked at him. Perhaps he was afraid she knew his thoughts. Did she?

"Then Abraham gave up the ghost, and died in a good old age, an old man, and full of years; and was gathered to his people.

"And his sons Isaac and Ishmael buried him in the cave of Machpelah, in the field of Ephron the son of Zohar the Hittite, which is before Manre.

"The field which Abraham purchased of the sons of Heth; there was Abraham buried, and Sarah his wife.

"And it came to pass after the death of Abraham, that God blessed his son Isaac; and Isaac dwelt by the well of Lahairoi."

.　　.　　.　　.　　.

It was a little odd that, in spite of all the things Fred had told her Aline couldn't get the figure of Old Grey, the banker, fixed in her mind. He had died just after Fred had married her, in Paris, and while Fred was hurrying home to him, leaving his new wife behind. It might have been that Fred did not want her to see the father, did not want the father to see her. He had just made a boat on the evening of the day he got the word of his father's illness and Aline did not sail until a month later.

He remained then, for Aline—"Old Grey"—a myth. Fred said he had lifted things up, had lifted the town up. It had been a mere mudhole village before his time, Fred said. "Now look at it." He had made the valley produce, he had made the town produce. Fred had been a fool not to see things clearer. He had stayed on in Paris after the war was over, hanging around, had even thought for a time he might go in for one of the arts, something of that sort. "In all France there never was such a man as father," Fred had once declared to his wife Aline. He was a bit too emphatic when he made such declarations. If he had not stayed on in Paris he would not have met Aline, would never have married her. When he made such statements Aline smiled, a soft knowing smile, and Fred changed his tone—a little.

There was that fellow he roomed with at college. The fellow was always talking and giving Fred books to read, books by George Moore, James Joyce—"The Artist as a Young Man." He had got Fred all balled up and he had even gone so far as to half defy his father about coming home; and then, when he saw his son's mind was made up, Old Grey had done what he had thought a shrewd thing. "You take a year in Paris, studying art, doing whatever you choose, and then you come home and have a year here with me," Old Grey had written. The son was to have whatever monies he wanted. Now Fred wished he had taken the first year at home. "I might have been some comfort to him. I was shallow and thoughtless. I might have met you, Aline, in Chicago, or in New York," Fred said.

What Fred had got out of the year in Paris was Aline. Was it worth the price? The old man living alone at home, waiting. He never even saw his son's wife, never even heard of her. A man with but one son, and that son in Paris, fooling around after the war was over, after he had done his share of the job, over there. Fred had a little knack for drawing, just

[162]

as Aline had, but what of that? He never even knew what he was after. Did Aline know what she was after? It would be nice if he could talk to Aline about it all. Why couldn't he? She was sweet and fine, very quiet most of the time. With such a woman you had to be careful.

. . . . .

The car was grinding its way up the hillside now. There was one short street, very steep and crooked, where you had to shift into low.

Men, working-men, advertising solicitors, business men. Fred's friend in Paris, the fellow who worked him up to defy his father and to try his hand at becoming a painter. He was a man who might very well turn out to be just such another fellow as Joe Walker. Already he was working Fred. Fred thought that he, Tom Burnside, his college friend, was everything a painter should be. He knew how to sit in a café, knew the names of wines, spoke French with an almost perfect Parisian accent. Pretty soon now he would begin to make trips to America to sell paintings and do portraits. Already he had sold Fred a painting for eight hundred dollars. "It's the best thing I've done so far and a man here wants to buy it for two thousand, but I don't want to quite have it pass out of my hands just yet. I would rather have it in your hands. My one true friend." Fred had fallen for that. Another Joe Walker. If he managed to pick himself up an Esther somewhere he would do well. Nothing like making a friend of some rich man while you are both

[163]

young. When Fred showed the painting to some of his friends in the town of Old Harbor, Aline had a kind of shaky feeling of being, not in the presence of a husband, but at home in the presence of her father—her father showing some fellow lawyer or a client the portraits Joe Walker had done.

If you are a woman why can't you get the man you have married as a child and be satisfied with that? Was it because a woman wanted her own children, did not want to adopt them, or marry them? Men, working-men, in her husband's factory, tall men, short men. Men walking along a Parisian boulevard at night. Frenchmen with a certain air. They were onto the women, the French. The idea was to stay on top of the heap, when women were concerned, use them, make them serve. Americans were sentimental fools about women. They wanted them to do for a man what he hadn't strength to try to do for himself.

The man at Rose Frank's apartment, that evening when she first met Fred. Why was he in some odd way different? Why had he stayed so sharply in Aline's mind all these months? Just seeing, on the streets of an Indiana town, a man who made the same sort of impression on the mind, had stirred her all up, set her mind and her fancy whirling. It had happened two or three times, in the evening when she drove down for Fred.

It might be that, on the night in Paris when she got Fred, she had wanted the other man instead.

He, the other man, she found at Rose's apartment,

when she went there with Esther and Joe, had paid no attention to her, hadn't even spoken to her.

The working-man she had just seen, walking up the hillside street with the short, broad-shouldered cocky-looking man, was like that other in some indefinable way. How absurd that she could not speak to him, find out something about him. She asked Fred who the short man was and he laughed. "That's Sponge Martin. He's a card," Fred said. He might have said more but he wanted to think of what the Chicago advertising man had told him. He was smart, that advertising man. Up to a game of his own all right, but if it fell in with Fred's game, what of it?

CHAPTER NINETEEN

AT Rose Frank's apartment in Paris, that evening, after the half-experience with Esther on the boat coming over and after some weeks among Esther's and Joe's acquaintances in Paris. The painter and his wife knew a good many rich Americans in Paris looking for an exciting time and Esther so managed it that she and Joe got in on a good many parties without spending much money. They added an artistic touch and also they were discreet—when discretion was wise.

And after the evening on the boat Esther felt more or less free with Aline. She gave Aline credit for more knowledge of life than she had.

That was something gained, for Aline, at least she thought it a gain. She had begun to move more freely within the circle of her own thoughts and impulses. Sometimes she thought—"Life is but a dramatization. You decide on your part in life and then try to play it skillfully." To play it badly, bunglingly, was the great sin. Americans in general, young men and women like herself who had money enough and social position enough to be secure, could do about as they pleased if they were careful about covering their trails. At home, in America, there was something in the very air you breathed that made you feel secure while at the same time it limited you terribly. Good and bad

were definite things, morality and immorality were definite things. You moved in a well-defined circle of
thoughts, ideas and emotions. Being a good woman
you got from men the respect they thought due a good
woman. Given money and a respectable position in life
you had to do openly something that defied openly the
social laws before you could step into a free world, and
the free world into which you stepped by any such
action was not free at all. It was dreadfully limited,
ugly in fact, the kind of world inhabited by—well, say,
by movie actresses.

In Paris, and rather in spite of Esther and Joe,
Aline had got a sharp sense of something in French
life that fascinated her. Little incidental things about
life, the men's comfort-stalls in the open streets, the
stallions hitched to dust-carts and trumpeting to mares,
lovers kissing each other openly in the streets in the
late afternoons—a kind of matter-of-fact acceptance
of life that the English and Americans seemed unable to come to, rather charmed her. Sometimes she
went with Esther and Joe to the Place Vendôme and
spent the day with their American friends, but more
and more she got into the habit of going off alone.

A woman unaccompanied in Paris always had to be
ready for annoyances. Men spoke to her, made sug-
gestive movements with their hands, their mouths,
followed her along the street. There was always going
on, whenever she went forth alone, a kind of attack
against herself, as a woman, as a being with woman's
flesh, woman's secret desires. If something was gained

by the frankness of Continental life there was also much lost.

She went to the Louvre. At home she had taken drawing and painting lessons at the Institute and had been called clever. Joe Walker had praised her work. Others had praised it. Then she had thought Joe must be a real painter. "I got caught by the American trick of thinking that what succeeded, was, for that reason, fine," she thought, and the thought, coming as her own and not having been forced upon her by another, was a revelation. Of a sudden she, the American, began walking in the presence of men's work feeling really humble. Joe Walker, all of his type of men, the successful painters, writers, musicians, who were America's heroes, got smaller and smaller in her eyes. Her own clever little imitative art seemed in the presence of work by El Greco, Cézanne, Fra Angelico and other Latins but child's prattling, and the American men who stood high in the history of America's attempts at the cultural life——?

There was Mark Twain, who wrote a book called "The Innocents Abroad," that Aline's father had loved. When she was a child he was always reading it and laughing with delight over it, and it had really been nothing but a kind of small boy's rather nasty disdain of things he couldn't understand. Pap for vulgar minds. Could Aline honestly think her father or Mark Twain were vulgar men? Well, she could not. To Aline her father had always been sweet, kind and tender—too tender perhaps.

One morning she sat on a bench in the Tuileries and

near her on another bench two young men were talking. They were French and had not seen her take a seat on the near-by bench, and they talked. It was good to hear such talk. A kind of intense fervor about the art of painting. What was the right road? One of them declared for the Moderns, for Cézanne and Matisse, and burst forth suddenly into warm hero-worship. The men of whom he was speaking had kept, all their lives, to the good road. Matisse was doing it yet. Such men had in them devotion, bigness, the grand manner. It had been pretty much lost to the world until they came, and now—after their coming and because of their fine devotion—it had a chance of really being born again into the world.

Aline on her bench had leaned forward to listen. The words of the young Frenchman, flowing rapidly forth, were a little hard to catch. Her own French was rather slipshod. She waited for each word, leaning forward. If such a man—if someone having such fervor for what he thought fine in life—if he could only be brought near herself——

And then, at that moment, the young man, seeing her, seeing the look on her face, got to his feet and started toward her. Something warned her. She would have to flee, get a taxicab. The man was after all a Continental. There was the touch of Europe, of the Old World, of a world in which men knew too much about women and not enough—perhaps. Were they right or wrong? There was an inability to think or feel women as anything but flesh, that was both terrible and in an odd way also true enough—to an American woman, to an English woman perhaps, too startling though. When Aline met such a man, in the company of Joe and Esther—as she sometimes did—when her position was well-defined, safe, he seemed, beside most American men she had ever known, altogether grown up, graceful in his approach to life, much more worth while, much more interesting, with infinitely greater capacity for accomplishment—real accomplishment.

.   .   .   .

As she walked with Esther and Joe, Esther kept pulling nervously at Aline. Her mind was filled with little hooks that wanted to grapple about in Aline's mind. "Have you been stirred or moved by life over here? Are you just a stupid, self-satisfied American woman looking for a man—thinking that settles anything? You go along—a prim, neat little figure of a woman, with good ankles, a small sharp interesting face, a good neck—the body graceful and fascinating too. What are you up to—really? Very soon now— within three or four years—your body will begin to settle into heaviness. Someone is going to tarnish your loveliness. I would rather like to do it. There would be satisfaction in that, a kind of joy. Do you think you can escape? Is that what you're up to—you little American fool?"

.   .   .   .

Esther walking through Parisian streets thinking. Joe, her husband, missing it all—not caring. He smoked cigarettes, twirled his cane. Rose Frank, to whose apartment they were going, was a correspondent

for several American newspapers that wanted a weekly
letter, gossip about Americans in Paris, and Esther
thought it just as well to keep in with her. If Rose
was onto Esther and Joe what did it matter? They
were of the sort American newspapers want to gossip
about.

· · · · ·

It was the night after the Quat'z Arts Ball, and as
soon as they had got to the apartment Aline knew
something was wrong, although Esther—not at the
moment so keen—did not sense it. She was perhaps
occupied with Aline, thinking of her. Already several
people had gathered, Americans all, and at once Aline,
who from the first was very sensitive to Rose and her
moods, concluded that, had she not already invited the
people to come to her on that particular evening, Rose
would have been glad to be alone or almost alone.

There was a studio apartment with a large room in
which the people had gathered, and Rose, the hostess,
was wandering about among them, smoking cigarettes
and with a queer vacant look in her eyes. When she
saw Esther and Joe she made a gesture with the hand
that held the cigarette. "Oh, Lord, you too, did I invite you?" the gesture seemed to say. At Aline she did
not at first look at all; but later, when several other
men and women had come in, she sat on a couch in a
corner still smoking the cigarettes and staring at Aline.

"Well, well, and so you are what you are? You
also are here? I do not remember ever to have met
you. You are with the Walker crew and so I fancy

you are newspaper stuff. Miss So-and-So of Indianapolis. Something of that sort. The Walkers take
no chances. When they tote anyone around it means
money for them."

Rose Frank's thoughts. She smiled as she looked
at Aline. "I've been up against something. I've been
banged. I'm going to talk. I've got to. It doesn't
much matter to me who is here. People have to take
their chances. Now and then something happens to a
human being—it might happen even to a rich young
American woman like you—something that lies too
heavy on the mind. When it happens you've got to
talk. You've got to explode. Look out, you! Something is going to happen to you, young lady, but I'm
not to blame. You're to blame for being here."

.   .   .   .

It was obvious something was wrong with the American newspaper woman. Everyone in the room felt it.
There was a hurried, rather nervous outbreak of talk,
all taking part in it except only Rose Frank, Aline and
a man who sat at the side of the room and who had not
noticed Aline, Joe, Esther or any of the others as they
came in. He spoke once, to a young woman who sat
near him. "Yes," he said, "I was there, lived there
for a year. I worked as a painter of bicycle wheels
in a factory there. It's about eighty miles from
Louisville, isn't it?"

.   .   .   .   .

It was the evening after the night of the Quat'z
Arts Ball of the year after the war's end, and Rose

Frank, having been to the ball with a young man—not present at her party on the following evening—wanted to talk of something that had happened to her.

"I'll have to talk about it, or I'll explode if I don't," she was saying to herself, as she sat in her apartment among her guests, staring at Aline.

.   .   .   .

She began. Her voice was highly pitched, filled with nervous excitement.

All of the others in the room, all who had been talking, stopped suddenly. There was an embarrassed hush. The people, men and women, had gathered in little groups, disposing of themselves in chairs drawn together and on a large couch in a corner. Several rather younger men and women sat in a circle on the floor. Aline, having, after that first look Rose had given them, instinctively moved away from Joe and Esther, sat alone on a chair near a window that looked down into a street. The window was open and as there was no screen she could see people moving about. Men and women moving down toward the rue Voltaire to cross one of the bridges into the Tuileries or to go sit in a café on the boulevards. Paris! Paris at night! The silent young man who did not speak, except for the one sentence about working in a bicycle factory somewhere in America, obviously in reply to a question, seemed to have some indefinable connection with Rose Frank. Aline kept turning her head to look at him and at Rose. Something was about to happen in the room, and there was a reason, that could not be explained, why it directly concerned the silent man, herself and the young man named Fred Grey who sat beside the silent man. "Perhaps he is like myself, doesn't know much," Aline thought, glancing at Fred Grey.

Four people, for the most part strangers to each other, oddly isolated in a roomful of people. Something was about to happen that concerned them as it could not concern any of the others. It was already happening. Did the silent man, sitting alone and looking at the floor, love Rose Frank? Could there be such a thing as love among such a congregation of people, Americans of that sort, gathered in a room in a Paris apartment—newspaper people, young radicals, art students? A queer notion that Esther and Joe should be there. They didn't fit in and Esther felt it. She was a little nervous, but her husband Joe—he took what followed as something delicious.

Four people, strangers to each other, isolated in a roomful of people. People were like drops of water in a river, flowing along. Suddenly the river became angry. It became furiously energetic, spreading out over lands, uprooting trees, sweeping houses away. Little whirlpools formed. Certain drops of water were whirled round and round in a circle, constantly touching each other, merging into each other, being absorbed into each other. There came times when human beings ceased being isolated. What one felt others felt. One might say that, at certain times, one left one's own body and went, quite completely, into the body of another. Love might be something like that. The silent man in the room seemed, as Rose Frank talked, to be a part of her. How odd!

And the young American—Fred Grey—he clung to Aline. "You are someone I can understand. I am out of my depths here."

.   .   .   .   .   .

A young Irish-American newspaper man, who had been sent by his American newspaper to Ireland to make a report on the Irish revolution and to interview the revolutionary leader, began to talk—insistently interrupting Rose Frank. "They took me in a cab blindfolded. I, of course, had no notion of where I was going. I had to trust the man and I did. The blinds were drawn. I kept thinking of that ride of Madame Bovary's through the streets of Rouen. The cab rattled over the cobblestones in darkness. Perhaps the Irish love the drama of it.

"And, then, there I was. I was in a room with him —with V——, who is being hunted so hard by the secret agents of the British government, sitting with him in a room, as tight and snug as two bugs in a rug. I got a great story. I'm going to hit for a raise."

.   .   .   .   .   .

It was an attempt—to stop Rose Frank talking.

Everyone in the room then had felt something wrong with the woman?

Having invited the others to her apartment for that particular evening she did not want them there. She did want Aline. She wanted the silent man sitting by himself and a young American named Fred Grey.

Why she wanted just those four people Aline couldn't have said. She felt it. The young Irish-American newspaper man had tried to speak of his experiences in Ireland to relieve a kind of tension in the room. "Now wait, you! I'll talk and then someone else will talk. We'll get through the evening comfortably and nicely. Something has happened. Perhaps Rose has quarreled with her lover. That man sitting over there alone may be her lover. I never saw him before but I'll bet he is. Give us a chance, Rose, and we'll get you through this bad moment." It was something of that sort the young man, by the telling of his tale, had been trying to say to Rose and the others.

.   .   .   .   .

It would not work. Rose Frank laughed, a queer high nervous laugh—dark laughter that. She was a plump strong-looking little American woman of perhaps thirty and was reputed to be very clever and able at her job.

"Well, the devil, I was there. I took part in it all, saw it all, felt it all," she said in a loud harsh voice and, although she had not said where she had been, everyone in the room, even Aline and Fred Grey knew what she meant.

.   .   .   .   .

It had been in the air for days—a promise, a threat—the Quat'z Arts Ball of that year, and had come off on the night before.

Aline had felt its coming in the air and so had Joe

[176]

and Esther. Joe had secretly wanted to go, had hungered to go.

.   .   .   .   .

The Quat'z Arts Ball of Paris is an institution. It is a part of student life in the capital of the arts. Every year it is held, and on that night the young art students, who have come to Paris from all over the Western world—from America, England, South America, Ireland, Canada, Spain—who have come to Paris to study one of the four very delicate arts—on that night they kick the roof off.

Delicacy of line, tenderness of line, color sensitiveness—for to-night—bah!

Women came—usually models from the studios—free women. Everyone goes the limit. That is expected. This once—anyway!

It happens every year, but in the year after the war's end—— Well, it was a year, wasn't it?

.   .   .   .   .

There had been something in the air for a long time.

For too long a time!

Aline had seen something of the blow-off in Chicago on the first Armistice Day and it had moved her strangely as it had all people who saw and felt it. There had been stories of the same sort of thing going on in New York, Cleveland, St. Louis, New Orleans—even in small American towns. Gray-haired women kissing boys, young women kissing young men—factories deserted—the lid off prohibition—offices empty —song—dance a little once again in life—you who haven't been in the war, in the trenches, you who are just tired of whooping it up for war, for hate—joy— grotesque joy. The lie given the lie.

The end of lies, the end of keeping up the pretense, the end of that sort of cheapness—the end of the War.

.   .   .   .   .

Men lying, women lying, children lying, being taught to lie.

Preachers lying, priests lying, bishops, popes and cardinals lying.

Kings lying, governments lying, writers lying, artists drawing lying pictures.

A debauch of lying. Keep it up! The bitter end! Outlast the other liar! Make him eat it! Kill. Kill some more! Keep on killing! Liberty! Love of God! Love of men! Kill! Kill!

.   .   .   .   .

The thing in Paris had been carefully thought out— planned. Had not the young artists of the world who came to Paris—to study there the very delicate arts— had they not gone into the trenches instead—for France —dear France? Mother of arts, eh? Young men— artists—the more sensitive men of the Western world——

.   .   .   .   .

Show 'em something! Show 'em up! Slap it into 'em!

Give 'em the limit!

They talk so big—make 'em like it!

.   .   .   .   .

Well, everything has gone to pot, the fields destroyed, the fruit-trees cut, the vines torn out of the ground, old Mother Earth herself given the riz-raz. Is this damn cheap civilization of ours to go blandly on, never getting a slap in the face? What t'ell?

Dada, eh? The innocents! Babes! Sweet womanhood! Purity! The hearth and home!

Choke the babe in the crib!

Bah, that isn't the way! Let's show 'em!

.   .   .   .   .

Slap it home to the women! Hit 'em where they live! Slap it home to the gabblers! Give 'em the riz-raz!

.   .   .   .   .

In the gardens in the cities, moonlight in the trees. You never were in the trenches, were you—a year, two years, three, four, five, six?

What t'ell moonlight?

.   .   .   .   .

Slap it to the women once! They were in it up to the neck. Sentimentality! Gush! That's what's back of it all—a lot anyway. They liked it all—the women. Give 'em a party once! *Cherchez la femme!* We were sold out, up to the hilt, and they helped, a lot. A lot of David and Uriah stuff, too. Bathshebas aplenty.

Women talked a lot about tenderness—"our beloved sons"—remember? French women whooping it up, English women, Irish, Italian. How come?

* * * * *

Roll 'em in the stench of it! Life! Western civilization!

Stench of the trenches—in the fingers, the clothes, the hair—staying there—getting into the blood—trench thoughts, trench feelings—trench love, eh?

Is not this dear Paris, the capital of our Western civilization?

What t'ell? Let's give 'em a look-in, once anyway!

* * * * *

Were we not what we were? Did we not dream? Did we not love a little, eh?

* * * * *

Nudity now!

Perversion—well, what of that?

Throw 'em on the floor, dance on 'em.

How good are you? How much you got left in you?

How come your eye out and your nose not skun?

* * * * *

All right. That little brown plump thing over there. Watch me. Keep your eyes on the trench-hound once!

Young artists of the Western world. Let's show 'em the Western world—this once!

The limit, eh—this once!

Do you like it—eh?

How come?

CHAPTER TWENTY

ROSE Frank, the American newspaper woman, had been to the Quat'z Arts Ball on the evening before Aline saw her. For several years, all through the war, she had made her living by sending smart Parisian gossip to American newspapers, but she also had hungered for—the limit. It was in the air just then, the hunger for the limit.

And on the evening in her apartment she had to talk. It was a mad necessity with her. Having been at the debauch all night she had been awake all day, walking up and down in her room and smoking cigarettes—waiting—to talk perhaps.

She had been through it all. It wasn't on the cards for newspaper men to get in, but a woman could work it—if she would take the chances.

Rose had gone with a young American art student, whose name she did not mention. When she had insisted the young American had laughed.

"All right. You fool! I'll do it."

The young American had said he would try to take care of her.

"I'll try to manage. We'll all be drunk of course."

. . . . . .

And after it was over, in the early morning, the two had gone for a ride to the Bois in a fiacre. The birds singing softly. Men, women and children walking along. An old gray-haired man—rather fine-looking— riding a horse in the park. He might have been a public man—member of the chamber of deputies or something of that sort. On the grass in the park a young boy, not over ten, was playing with a small white dog, while a woman stood in a near-by path watching. There was a soft little smile on her lips. The boy had such fine-looking eyes.

.   .   .   .   .

Oh, Lord!
Oh, Kalamazoo!

.   .   .   .   .

It takes a long, lean
    brown-skin gal
To make a preacher lay
    his Bible down.

.   .   .   .

But what an experience it was! It had taught Rose something. What? She did not know.

What she was sorry for—ashamed of—was that she had put the young American to a world of trouble. After she got there and it was going on, everywhere, everything whirled around—she got dizzy, faint.

And then desire—black, ugly, hungry desire—like a desire to kill everything that ever had been lovely in the world—in herself and others—everyone.

She danced with a man who tore her dress open. She did not care. The young American came running and snatched her away. It happened three, four, five times, things like that. She could not remember. The other men were all drunk and the young American drank nothing. He didn't even smoke cigarettes. There was a reason. It did not matter.

Esther sat back of Aline looking a little nervous and upset, like one on a ship in a storm, as Rose talked; but Joe fairly licked his chops. He wasn't very pleasant to look at while Rose was talking.

When she talked, sometimes Rose laughed, sometimes there were tears in her eyes. "I'll never talk about it again, after this once," she said.

What seemed to hurt her most was that she had come out of it physically untouched, had escaped. "Such cheating when I felt that way inside! Mud! Muddy men! Muddy women! The war! Why should I have escaped?"

Once the Irish-American newspaper man tried to interrupt.

"In Ireland," he said, and then began again.

"In Ireland——"

He stopped.

.   .   .   .   .

"The fight for Irish freedom is going to go on."

.   .   .   .   .

The pantomimes began at twelve, Rose said—twenty-nine ways of love-making—all done in the life—naked people. There was a moment. At twelve any woman who wanted to save herself could get out. After that all barriers down. "I stuck."

"There was something to decide. There was everything to decide. The youngster I went with had said he would try to see me through. What t'ell about him? Did I want to cramp his style?

"Such a strange feeling in me—something primitive like a nigger woman in an African dance. That was what they were after when they got up the show. You strip all away, no pretense. If I'd been a nigger woman —good night—something exotic. No chance then— that's sure.

"Take a woman like me. I've been about a little. A newspaper woman sees things. Suppose something, your thoughts—we all have—that we are ashamed of —all the thoughts and strange terrible dreams you have when you're a young girl—say fifteen at night— when the bed is hot—you can't sleep—you can't come awake—all that stripped bare.

"All your thoughts acted out by humans—men and women, right before your eyes, showing yourself up to yourself—for once—something like that. Most of the women who stayed didn't care. It was a man's orgy, that one. Men doing something to show women up, for their gush—sentimentality—make 'em muddy— make 'em reek with it—something of that sort. Could a woman subscribe to it, fall into the swing of it? Plenty did. I saw things. They liked it. I myself escaped, by a lucky fluke, by cheating, as always. That kid who went with me. When a man grabbed me he always appeared and snatched me away. Everyone was pretty drunk. That saved me if I was saved. Can anyone be saved in this world?

[184]

"A kind of swoon, an orgy, a wild untamable thing. Most of the men there were young fellows who had been in the trenches, for France, for America, for England, you know. France for preservation, England for control of the seas, America for souvenirs. They were getting their souvenirs fast enough. They had got cynical—didn't care. If you're here and you are a woman, what you doing here? I'll show you. Damn your eyes. If you want to fight, all the better. I'll slug you. That's a way of making love. Didn't you know?

"The kid took me for the ride afterward. It was early morning and up in the Bois the trees were green and the birds were singing. Such thoughts in the head, things the kid with me had seen, things I had seen. The kid with me was fine, laughing. He had been in the trenches two years. 'Sure we kids can stand a war. What t'ell. We got to stand for people all our lives, ain't we?' He thought of the green things, kept getting himself out of the riz-raz that way. 'You let yourself in for it. I told you, Rose,' he said. He might have taken me like a sandwich, consumed me, eaten me up, I mean. What he told me was good sense. 'Don't try to go to sleep to-day,' he said.

" 'I've seen this,' he said. 'What of it? Let her ride. It doesn't jar me no more than I've been jarred, but now I don't think you had better see me any more to-day. You might get to hate me. You get to hate all people in war—and in things like this. It doesn't matter that nothing happened to you, that you slid out. That doesn't cut any figure. Don't let it make you

[185]

ashamed. Count it that you married me and found you didn't want me or that I didn't want you, something of that sort.' "

.   .   .   .   .

Rose had stopped talking. She had been walking nervously up and down the room and smoking cigarettes as she talked. When the words stopped coming from her lips she dropped into a chair and sat with the tears running down her plump cheeks, and several of the women in the room went and tried to comfort her. They seemed to want to kiss her. One by one several women went to her and leaning over kissed her hair, but Esther and Aline sat each in her place with her hands gripped. What it meant to the one it did not mean to the other, but they were both upset. "A fool, that woman, for letting anything get her like that, for getting upset and giving herself away," Esther would have said.

BOOK SEVEN

CHAPTER TWENTY-ONE

THE Greys, Fred and Aline, having driven up the hill to their house in Old Harbor, had dined. Was Aline doing to her husband Fred the same little trick Bruce had been in the habit of doing to his wife Bernice in the Chicago apartment? Fred Grey spoke of his affairs, of the plan to advertise in magazines with a national circulation the wheels made in his factory.

For him, the wheel factory had become the center of life. There he moved about, a little king in a world of smaller officials, clerks and workers. The factory and his position meant even more to him because of his experience as a private in the army during the war. At the factory something within him seemed to expand. It was, after all, a huge plaything, a world set apart from the town—a walled town within the confines of a town—in which he was ruler. Did the men want a day off because of the celebration of some national holiday —Armistice Day, something of that sort—he was the one to say "Yes" or "No." One was a bit careful not to get chesty. Often Fred said to Harcourt, who was secretary of the company—"I am, after all, but a servant." It was good occasionally to say such things, to remind oneself of the responsibility that must be shouldered by the man of affairs, responsibility to property, to other investors, to workmen, to workmen's families. Fred had a hero—Theodore Roosevelt. What a shame he was not at the helm during the World War. Had not Roosevelt had things to say about men of wealth who did not shoulder the responsibility of position? Had Teddy been in there at the beginning of the World War, we would have got in quicker—smashed 'em.

The factory was a little kingdom, but what about Fred's home? He was a little nervous about his position there. That smile his wife wore sometimes when he spoke of his affairs. What did she mean by it?

Fred thought he ought to talk.

We have a market for all the wheels we can make now, but things may change. The question is—does the average man who runs an automobile know or care where the wheels come from? It's a thing to think about. It costs a lot of money to advertise nationally, but if we don't do it we will have to pay a lot more taxes—surplus earnings, you know. The government lets you deduct what you spend for advertising. What I mean is, that they let you count it as legitimate expense. The newspapers and magazines have a lot of power, I tell you. They weren't going to let the government take that snap away. Well, I suppose I might as well do it.

Aline sat smiling. Fred always thought she looked more like a European woman than an American. When she smiled like that and did not say anything, was she laughing at him? Damn it all, the whole matter of whether the wheel company made money or not was as important to her as to himself. She had always

been used to nice things, as a child and after her marriage. Lucky for her the man she had married had
plenty of money. Aline spent thirty dollars a pair for
shoes. Her feet were long and narrow, and it was
difficult to get custom-made shoes that did not hurt her
feet, so she ordered them made. There must be twenty
pairs in the closet of her room upstairs, and they had
cost her thirty to forty dollars a pair. Two times three
is six. Six hundred dollars for shoes alone. Good
Lord!

Maybe she didn't mean anything special by that smile.
Fred suspected that his affairs, the affairs of the factory, were a little over Aline's head. Women didn't
care for or understand such things. It took a man's
brain for that. Everyone had thought he, Fred Grey,
would make a mess of his father's affairs when he was
suddenly called upon to take charge, but he hadn't.
As for woman, he didn't want one of the smart-man-
aging sort, one of the kind who try to tell you how to
run things. Aline suited him all right. He wondered
why he hadn't any children. Was it her fault or his?
Well, she was in one of her moods. When she was
that way you might as well let her alone. She would
come out of it after a while.

When the Greys had dined, Fred rather insistently
keeping up the conversation about national advertising
of automobile wheels, he wandered into the living-room
of the house to sit in an easy chair under a lamp and
read the evening paper while he smoked a cigar and
Aline slipped unseen away. There had come a stretch
of unusually warm days for that time of the year, and

she put a cloak about her and walked out into the garden. Nothing growing yet. The trees still bare. She sat on a bench and lighted a cigarette. Fred, her husband, liked her smoking. He thought it gave her rather an air—of Europe perhaps—of class, anyway.

In the garden the soft dampness of a late winter—or early spring night. Which was it? The seasons hung balanced. How very quiet everything in the garden on the hilltop! There was no doubt the Middle West was isolated from the world. In Paris, London, New York—now at this hour—people getting ready to drive out to the theater. Wine, lights, the swirl of people, talk. You get caught up, carried along. No time to get immeshed in a whirlpool of your own thoughts—thoughts driving through you like raindrops, wind-driven.

Too many thoughts!

That night when Rose talked—the intensity of it, that had caught Fred and Aline, that had played with them as a wind plays with dry, dead leaves—the war—the ugliness of it—men drenched with ugliness like rain—years of that.

The Armistice—release—the attempt at naked joy.

Rose Frank talking—the flood of naked words—dancing. After all, most of the women at the ball in Paris were what? Whores? An attempt to throw off pretense, fakiness. So much fake talk during the war. The war for righteousness—to make the world Free. The young men sick, sick, and sick of it. Laughing, though—dark laughter. Taking it standing up—the men. The words Rose Frank had said—about her shame—that she had not gone the limit—in ugliness. Queer, disconnected thoughts, women's thoughts. You want a man, but you want the best of the lot—if you can get him.

There was that young Jewish man who talked to Aline one evening in Paris after she married Fred. He had for an hour got into the same mood Rose had been in and that Fred got into—just once—that time he asked Aline to marry him. She smiled at the thought. The young American Jew, who was a connoisseur of prints and had a valuable collection, had escaped going down into the trenches. "What I did was to dig latrines—it seemed to me thousands of miles of latrines. Digging, digging, digging in a rocky soil —trenches—latrines. They got the habit of making me do that. I was trying to write music when the war began; that is to say, when they raked me in. I thought —'Well, a sensitive man, a neurotic,' I thought. I thought they would pass me up. Every man, not a silly blind fool, thought that, hoped that, whether he said it or not. Anyway, he hoped. For once it was grand to be a cripple, or blind, or have diabetes. There was such a lot of it, drilling, the ugly shacks we lived in, no privacy, finding out too much about your fellow men too fast. Latrines. Then it was over, and I did not try to write music any more. I had some money, and I started to buy prints. I wanted things delicate— delicacy of line and feeling—something outside myself more delicate and sensitive than I could ever be—after what I had been through."

Rose Frank went to that ball where things blew off.

No one afterward in Aline's presence talked much about it. Rose was an American and she escaped. She escaped getting clear into it, up to the limit, slid through —thanks to that kid who took care of her—an American kid.

Had Aline slipped through, too? Had Fred, her husband, slipped through untouched? Was Fred the same thing he would have been if the war had never come, thinking the same thoughts, taking life the same way?

That night, after they all got out of Rose Frank's place, Fred had been drawn to Aline—as by instinct. He had come out of the place with Esther, Joe and herself. Perhaps, after all, Esther had gathered him in, having something in mind. "All is grist that comes to mill"—something like that. That young man who sat near Fred and said that about working in a factory in America before Rose began talking. He had stayed when the others got out. Being in Rose's apartment that night was, for all the people who had been there, a good deal like walking into a bedroom in which a woman lies naked. They had all felt that.

Fred had walked with Aline when they left the apartment. What had happened had drawn him to her, had drawn her to him. There was never any doubt of their closeness to each other—for that one night, anyway. He was to her, that evening, like the American kid who went with Rose to the ball, only nothing happened between them that was anything like what Rose had described.

Why hadn't something happened? If Fred had

[194]

wanted—that night. He hadn't. They had just walked along through the streets, Esther and Joe ahead somewhere, and then presently they lost Esther and Joe. If Esther felt any responsibility for Aline, she wasn't worried. She knew who Fred was if Aline did not. Trust Esther to know about a young man who had as much money as Fred. She was a regular hound-dog at spotting that kind. And Fred had also known who she was, that she was the respectable daughter of, oh, such a respectable Chicago attorney! Was that the reason——? How many things to ask Fred that she never had asked, couldn't—now that she was his wife —in Old Harbor, Indiana.

.   .   .   .   .

Both Fred and Aline had been shaken by what they had heard. They went along the left bank of the Seine and found a little café where they stopped and had a drink. When they had taken the drink, Fred looked at Aline. He was rather pale. "I don't want to appear greedy, but I want several stiff drinks—brandy—one right on top of the other. Do you mind if I take them?" he asked. Then they wandered along the Quai Voltaire, and crossed the Seine at the Pont Neuf. Presently they had got into the little park in the rear of Notre Dame de Paris. That she had never before seen the man she was with had seemed good to Aline that night and she had kept thinking: "If he wants any-thing, I can——" He had been a soldier—a private in the trenches for two years. Rose had made Aline feel so vividly the shame of escape when the world is plunged—into mud. That he had never before seen the woman he was with seemed good to Fred Grey that night. He had a notion about her. Esther had told him something. Just what Fred's notion had been, Aline had not understood—not then.

In the little park-like place into which they had wandered, French people of the neighborhood, young lovers, old men with their wives, fat middle-class men and women with children sitting about. Babies lying on the grass, their little fat legs kicking, women nursing babies, babies crying, a stream of talk, French talk. There was something Aline had once heard a man say concerning the French—when she was out for an evening with Esther and Joe. "They may be killing men in a battle, bringing in the dead from a battlefield, making love—it doesn't matter. When it comes time to sleep, they sleep. When it comes time to eat, they eat."

It had really been Aline's first night in Paris. "I want to stay out all night. I want to think and feel things. Maybe I want to get drunk," she had said to Fred.

Fred had laughed. As soon as he got alone with Aline he had begun to feel strong and manly, and it was, he thought, a good feeling. The shakiness inside had begun to go away. She was an American woman, one of the sort he would marry when he got back to America—which would be soon now. To have stayed on in Paris had been a mistake. There were too many things to remind you of what life was like when you saw it raw.

What one wanted from woman was not a conscious participation in the facts of life—its vulgarities. Plenty of that sort of women about—in Paris, anyway—Americans, a lot of them—Rose Frank and her sort. Fred had only gone to Rose Frank's apartment because Tom Burnside took him there. Tom came from good people in America, but thought—because he was in Paris and because he was a painter—well, he thought he ought to stick around with a lot of loose-living people—Bohemians.

The thing was to explain to Aline, make her understand. What? Well, that nice people—women, anyway—know nothing of the sort of things Rose had talked about.

The three or four shots of brandy Fred had taken had steadied him. In the dim light in the little park back of the cathedral he kept looking at Aline—at her sharp, delicate, small features, her slender feet, clad in expensive shoes, the slender hands lying in her lap. In Old Harbor, where the Greys had the brick house in the garden set on the very top of the hill above the river, how exquisite she would be—like one of the small, old-fashioned white marble statues people used to set on pedestals among green foliage in a garden.

The thing was to tell her—an American woman—pure and fine—what? What an American, such an American as himself, who had seen what he had seen in Europe, what such a man wanted. Why, on the very night before the one when he sat with Aline he had seen—Tom Burnside had taken him to a place on Montmartre to see Parisian life. Such women! Ugly women, ugly men—pandering to American men, English men.

That Rose Frank! Her outbreak—such sentiments, to come from a woman's lips.

"I've something to say to you," Fred had finally managed to speak.

"What?" Aline asked.

Fred tried to explain. Something he felt. "I've seen too many things like that Rose blowout," he said. "I've been up front."

In reality it had been Fred's intention to say something about America and the life at home—to remind her. There was something he felt needed reasserting to a young woman like Aline—to himself, too—something not to be forgotten. The brandy made him a bit loquacious. Names floated before his mind—names of men who stood for something in American life. Emerson, Benjamin Franklin, W. D. Howells—"The better aspects of our American life"—Roosevelt, the poet Longfellow.

"Truth, liberty—the freedom of man. America, mankind's great experiment in Liberty."

Was Fred drunk? He thought certain words and said other words. That fool woman—hysterical—talking back there in that apartment.

Thoughts dancing in the brain—horror. One night, in the time of the fighting, he went out on patrol in No Man's Land and saw another man stumbling along in darkness and shot him. The man pitched forward dead. It had been the only time Fred consciously killed a man. You don't kill men in war much. They just die. The act was rather hysterical on his part. He and the men with him might have made the fellow surrender. They had all got the jimjams. After it happened, they all ran away together.

A man killed. They rot sometimes, lying like that in shell-holes. You go out to gather them up, and they fall to pieces.

Once later Fred crawled out during an advance and got into a shell-hole. A fellow lying there, face down. Fred had crawled in close beside him and had asked him to move over a little. Move, hell! The man was dead—rotten with death.

Might have been the very fellow he shot that night when he was hysterical. How could he tell whether the fellow was a German or not—in darkness that way? He had got hysterical, that time.

Other times, before an advance. The men praying, speaking of God.

Then it was over and he and others were still alive. Other men living—as he was—rotten with life.

The strange desire for nastiness—on the tongue. To say words that reeked and stank as trenches stank—a madness for that—after such an escape—an escape with life—precious life—life to be nasty with, ugly with. Swear—curse God—go the limit.

America—far off. Something sweet and fine. You've got to believe in that—in the men there—the women there.

Hang on! Grip it with your fingers, your soul! Sweetness and truth! It's got to be sweet and true. Fields—cities—streets—houses—trees—women.

Specially women. Kill anyone who says anything against our women—fields—cities.

Specially women. They don't know what's up to them.

We're tired—damn tired, aching tired.

. . . . .

Fred Grey talking one night in a little park in Paris. At night on the roof of Notre Dame angels may be seen walking up into the sky—white-clad women—stepping up to God.

It may have been Fred was drunk. Perhaps Rose Frank's words had made him drunk. What was the matter with Aline? She cried. Fred clung to her. He did not kiss her, did not want that. "I want you to marry me—live with me in America." When he raised his head he could see the white-stone women—angels—walking up into the sky, on the roof of the cathedral.

Aline—to herself—"Woman? If he wants anything—he is a man hurt, befouled—why should I cling to myself?"

Rose Frank's words in Aline's mind, an impulse, Rose Frank's shame that she had remained—what is called clean.

Fred had begun to sob as he tried to talk to Aline, and she took him into her arms. The French people in the little park did not mind much. They had seen a lot of things—shell-shock—all that sort of thing—modern war. Getting late. Time to go home and sleep. French prostitution during the war. "They never forgot to ask for the money—did they, Buddy?"

Fred clung to Aline and Aline clung to Fred—that night. "You are a nice girl, I spotted you. That woman you were with told me, Tom Burnside introduced me to her. I'm all right at home—nice people. I've got to have you. We've got to believe in things—kill people who don't believe."

They went to ride in a fiacre—all night—to the Bois in the early morning—as Rose Frank and her American kid had done. After that a marriage—it had seemed inevitable.

Like a train when you are on and it starts. You got to go somewhere.

More talk. "Talk, boy—it helps maybe." Talk of a man killed—in the darkness. I'm too full of haunts, I don't want more talk. We Americans were all right. Getting along. Why did I stay here when the war was over? Tom Burnside got me to—for you, maybe. Tom never was in the trenches—lucky dog, I don't hold it against him.

"I want no more Europe-talk. I want you. You marry me. You got to. All I want is to forget—wade out. Let Europe rot."

Aline rode all night in the fiacre with Fred. It was such a courtship. He clung to her hand, but did not kiss her, and said nothing tender.

He was like a child, wanting something she stood for—to him—wanting it desperately.

Why not give herself? He was young and handsome.

She had been willing to give——
He had not seemed to want—that.

.　　.　　.　　.　　.

You get what you reach out your hand and take.
Women always do the taking—if they have the courage.
You take—a man—or a mood—or a child that has
been hurt too much. Esther was as hard as nails, but
she knew some things. It had been educational for
Aline to go to Europe with her. There wasn't much
doubt that Esther felt the outcome of her having thrown
Fred and Aline together was a triumph for her system,
for her way of managing things. She knew who Fred
was. It would be a feather in her cap, with Aline's
father, when he realized what she had done. Had he
had the picking of a husband for his daughter he
would have picked—just Fred. Not many of that kind
lying about loose. With such a man a woman—like
Aline would be when she had grown a little wiser and
older—well, she could manage just anything. She
also would be grateful to Esther, after a while.

And that was why Esther put the marriage right
through, the next day—the same day, to be exact. "If
you are going to keep a woman like that out all night—
young man." It had not been very hard to manage
Fred and Aline. Aline had seemed in a daze. She had
been in a daze. All that night and the next day and
for several days afterward she wasn't herself. What
was she? Perhaps she had been for the time, in fancy,
that newspaper woman, Rose Frank. The woman had
befuddled her—made all life seem strange and topsy-

turvy for the time being. Rose had given her the war, the sense of it—all in a heap—like a blow.

She—Rose—had been in something and had escaped. She was ashamed of her escape.

Aline wanted to be in something—up to the hilt— the limit—once, anyway.

She had got into——

A marriage with Fred Grey.

CHAPTER TWENTY-TWO

IN the garden Aline arose from the bench on which she had been sitting for a half hour, perhaps for an hour. The night was full of the promise of spring. In another hour her husband would be ready to go to bed. It had perhaps been a hard day for him at the factory. She would go into the house. No doubt he would have gone to sleep in his chair and she would arouse him. There would be some talk. "Are things going well at the factory?" "Yes, dear. I am very busy these days. Now I am trying to decide about advertising. Sometimes I think I will do it, sometimes I think I won't."

Aline would be alone in the house with the man, her husband, and outside would be the night of which he seemed so unconscious. When spring had advanced but a few weeks more, tender green growth would be springing up all over the hillside on which the house stood. The soil was rich up there. Fred's grandfather, still spoken of by old men of the town as Old Wash Grey, had been a horse-dealer on rather a grand scale. It was said he had sold horses to both sides during the Civil War, and had taken something of a hand in several big horse-running raids. He sold horses to Grant's army, there was a rebel raid, the horses disappeared and presently Old Wash sold them to Grant's army again. The whole hillside had once been a huge horse corral.

A place of green things growing rank in the spring— trees putting forth leaves, grasses springing up, the early spring flowers coming, flowering bushes every- where.

In the house, after the few remarks, silence. Aline and her husband would go up a flight of stairs. Always, when they had got to the top of the steps, there was a moment when something was to be decided. "Shall I come to you to-night?" "No, dear; I'm a little tired." Something hung fire between the man and woman, a wall separated them. It had always been there—except once, for an hour, one night in Paris. Did Fred really want to tear it away? To do so would involve something. Really living with a woman is not living alone. Life takes on a new aspect. There are new problems. You must feel things, face things. Aline wondered if she wanted the wall destroyed. Sometimes she made an effort. At the top of the stairs she turned and smiled at her husband. Then she took his head in her two hands and kissed him, and when she had done that went quickly into her own room, where later, in the darkness, he came to her. It was odd, amazing, how close another could come and yet remain far away. Could Aline, if she willed it so, knock the wall down and really come close to the man she had married? Did she want that?

It was so good to be out alone on such an evening as the one during which we have crept into Aline's thoughts. In the garden, that had been terraced over the crown of the hill on which the house stood, there were several trees with benches beneath, and a low wall that separated the garden from the street that went past the house over the hill and down again. In the summer when the trees were in leaf and when tall bushes grew thick upon the terraces one could not see the other houses of the street, but now they stood distinctly forth. In a neighboring house, where lived Mr. and Mrs. Willmott, there were guests in for the evening, and two or three motors stood before the door. The people sat at tables in a brightly lighted room playing cards. They laughed, talked, occasionally got up from one table and went to another. Aline had been invited to come with her husband, but had managed to get out of it by saying she had a headache. Slowly, surely, ever since she had been in Old Harbor, she had been restricting her own and her husband's social life. Fred said he liked it so and complimented her upon her ability to get out of things. In the evening after dinner he read the newspaper or a book. He preferred detective stories, saying he got a kick out of them and that they did not take his mind off business, as reading so-called serious books did. Sometimes he and Aline went for a drive in the evening, but not often. She had managed to restrict the mutual use of the car also. It threw her too much with Fred. There was nothing to talk about.

When Aline got up from her seat on the bench, she walked slowly and softly about the garden. She was dressed in white and there was a little childish game she loved playing with herself. She went to stand near a tree and, folding her arms, turned her face demurely toward the ground, or, plucking a branch from a bush, stood holding it against her breast as though it were a cross. In old gardens in Europe and in some old American places, where there are trees and thick bushes, a certain effect is achieved by setting small white figures on columns among the deep foliage, and Aline in fancy metamorphosed herself into such a white, dainty figure. She was a stone woman leaning over to raise to her arms a small child who stood with upraised hands, or she was a nun in the garden of a convent pressing a cross against her breast. As such a tiny stone figure she had no thoughts, no feelings. What she achieved was a kind of occasional loveliness among the dark night foliage of the garden. She became a part of the loveliness of the trees and of thick bushes growing out of the ground. Although she did not know it, her husband Fred had once in fancy seen her just so—on the night when he had asked her to marry him. For years, for days and nights, forever perhaps, she could stand with outstretched arms about to take a child into her arms, or as a nun holding to her body the symbol of the cross on which had died her spiritual lover. It was a dramatization, childish, meaningless, and full of a kind of comforting satisfaction to one who in the actuality of life remains unfulfilled. Sometimes when she stood thus in the garden, her husband within the house reading his paper or asleep in his chair, minutes passed when she did no thinking, felt nothing. She had become a part of the sky, of the ground, of passing winds. When it rained, she was the rain. When thunder rolled down the Ohio River Valley, her body trembled slightly. As a small, lovely stone figure, she had achieved Nirvana. Now was the time for her lover to come—to spring out of the ground —to drop from the branches of a tree—to take her, laughing at the very notion of asking consent. Such a figure as Aline had become, placed in an exhibition in a museum would have seemed absurd; but in a garden among trees and bushes, and caressed by the low color-tones of the night, it became strangely lovely, and all of Aline's relations with her husband had made her want, above everything else, to be strange and lovely in her own sight. Was she saving herself for something, and, if so, for what?

When she had posed herself thus, several times, she grew weary of the childishness of the game and was compelled to smile at her own foolishness. She went back along the path toward the house and, looking through a window, saw her husband asleep in his chair. The newspaper had fallen from his hand and his body had slumped into the chair's generous depths so that only his rather boyish-looking head was visible, and after looking at him for a moment Aline moved again along a path toward the gate leading to the street. Where the Grey place faced the street there were no houses. Two roads, coming up from the town below, became a street near the corner of the garden, and on the street were several houses, in one of which she could, by raising her eyes, see the people still at their card game.

Near the gate there was a large walnut-tree, and she

stood with her body pressed against it looking out into the street. At the corner, where the two roads joined, there was a street light, but at the entrance to the Grey place the light was dim.

Something happened.

A man came up the road from below, passed under the light and, turning, walked toward the Grey gate. It was Bruce Dudley, the man she had seen walking away from the factory with the small, broad-shouldered workman. Aline's heart jumped and then seemed to stop beating. If the man, inside himself, had been occupied with thoughts of her as she had with thoughts of him, then already they were something to each other. They were something to each other that presently would have to be taken into account.

The man in Paris, the one she had seen in Rose Frank's apartment that night when she got Fred. She had made a faint little try for him, but had been unsuccessful. Rose had got him. If the chance came again, would she be more bold? There was one thing sure—if such a thing did happen, her husband Fred would not be taken into account. "When such a thing happens between a woman and a man, it happens between a woman and a man. No one else really gets into it at all," she thought, smiling in spite of the fear that had taken hold of her.

The man she now stood watching was coming along the street directly toward her, and when he had got to the gate leading up into the Grey garden he stopped. Aline moved slightly, but a bush growing near the tree hid her body. Did the man see her? An idea came.

She would try, to some purpose now, being one of the small stone statues people place in gardens. The man worked in her husband's factory and it might well be that he was coming to the house to see Fred about business. Aline's notions of the relation between employee and employer in a factory were very vague. If the man actually came along the path toward the house, he would pass near enough to touch her, and the situation might well become absurd. It would have been better for Aline to walk quite nonchalantly along the path away from the gate at which the man now stood. That she realized, but she did not move. If the man saw her and spoke to her, the tenseness of the moment would be broken. He would ask something about her husband and she would answer. The whole childish game she had been playing inside herself would end. As a bird crouches in the grass when a hunting dog runs through a field so Aline crouched.

The man stood some ten feet away, looking first at the lighted house above and then calmly at her. Did he see her? Was he aware of her awareness? When the hunting dog has found his bird he does not dash in, but stands rigid and waiting.

.   .   .   .   .

How absurd that Aline could not speak to the man in the road. She had been thinking of him for days. Perhaps he had been thinking of her.

She wanted him.

For what?

She did not know.

[210]

He stood for three or four minutes, and it seemed to Aline one of those strange pauses in life that are so absurdly unimportant and at the same time all-important. Had she the courage to step out of the shelter of the tree and the bush and speak to him? "Something would then begin. Something would then begin." The words danced in her head.

He turned and walked away reluctantly. Twice he stopped to look back. First his legs, then his body, and at the last his head disappeared into the darkness of the hillside beyond the circle of light cast by the street-lamp overhead. There was an effect of sinking into the ground out of which he had suddenly appeared but a few moments before.

The man had stood as close to Aline as the other man in Paris, the man she had met coming out of Rose's apartment, the man on whom she had once tried with so little success to exert her womanly charms.

The new man's coming, in just that way, was a challenge.

Would she take it?

With a smile playing about her lips Aline walked along the path toward the house and toward her husband, who was still sound asleep in his chair with the evening newspaper lying beside him on the floor.

BOOK EIGHT

BOOK EIGHT

CHAPTER TWENTY-THREE

SHE had got him. There remained little doubt in his mind; but because it gave him a kind of pleasure to think of himself as the devoted one, and of her as indifferent, he did not tell himself the exact truth. However, it had happened. When he saw it all fully he smiled and was rather happy. "That is settled anyway," he told himself. It was flattering to think that he could do it, that he could surrender like that. One of the things Bruce said to himself at that time went something like this—"A man must at some time in his life focus all the strength of his being upon some one thing, the doing of some job of work, utter absorption in that or in some other human being, for a time anyway." All his life Bruce had been rather like that. When he felt closest to people they seemed more removed than when he felt—as rarely happened—sufficient unto himself. It needed then a grand effort, an outgoing toward someone.

As for work Bruce did not feel himself artist enough to think he would find an outlet in the arts. Now and then, when he was deeply moved, he wrote what might have been called poems, but the idea of being a poet, of being known as a poet, was rather dreadful to him. "Something like being widely known as a lover, a professional lover," he thought.

Ordinary work, varnishing wheels in a factory, scribbling news for a newspaper, that sort of thing. Not much chance for an outpouring of the emotional nature at least. Men like Tom Wills and Sponge Martin had puzzled him. They were shrewd, moved about within a certain limited circle of life with an air of ease. Perhaps they did not want or need what Bruce wanted and thought he needed—periods of rather intense emotional outpourings. Tom Wills at least had consciousness of futility, impotence. He used to talk with Bruce sometimes about the newspaper on which they both worked. "Think of it, man," he said, "three hundred thousand readers. Think what that means. Three hundred thousand pairs of eyes fixed on the same page at practically the same hour every day, three hundred thousand minds supposed to be at work absorbing the contents of a page. And such a page, such stuff. If they were really minds what would happen? Great God! An explosion that would shake the world, eh? If the eyes saw! If the fingers felt, if the ears heard! Man is dumb, blind, deaf. Could Chicago or Cleveland, Pittsburgh, Youngstown or Akron—modern war, the modern factory, the modern college, Reno, Los Angeles, movies, art schools, music-teachers, the radio, governments—could such things go on blandly if the three hundred thousand, all the three hundred thousands, were not intellectual and emotional morons?"

As though that mattered to Bruce or to Sponge Martin. It seemed to matter a lot to Tom. He was hurt by the fact.

Sponge was the puzzle. He went fishing, drank

moon whisky, got satisfaction out of being aware. He
and his wife were both fox terriers, not quite human.

Aline had got Bruce. The mechanics of getting
him, her move, had been laughable, crude, almost like
putting an advertisement in a matrimonial paper.
When she had realized fully that she wanted him near
her, for a time anyway, wanted his person near her
person, she could not think at first of any way to bring
it about. She couldn't very well send a note to his
hotel. "You look rather like a man I once saw in Paris,
give me the same subtle desires. I missed out on him.
A woman named Rose Frank got the better of me the
only chance I ever had. Would you mind coming a
bit nearer so that I may see what you are like?"

You can't do a thing like that in a small town. If
you are an Aline you can't do it at all. What can you
do?

Aline had taken a long chance. A negro gardener,
who worked about the Grey place, was discharged and
she put an advertisement in the local newspaper. Four
men came and were pronounced unsatisfactory before
she got Bruce, but in the end she got him.

It was an embarrassing moment when he came up the
path to the door and for the first time she saw him
very near, heard his voice.

That was in a way the test. Would he make it easy
for her? He at least tried, smiling inwardly. Something was dancing within him as it had since he had
seen the advertisement. He had seen it because two
laborers at the hotel spoke of it in his hearing. Suppose you play with the idea that a game is going on

between you and a very charming woman. Most men spend their lives at just that game. You tell yourself many little lies, but perhaps you are wise to do so. You've got to have some illusions, haven't you? It's fun, like writing a novel. You make the charming woman more charming if your fancy can be made to help, make her do as you please, have imaginary conversations with her, at night sometimes imagined love-meetings. That is not quite satisfactory. There isn't, however, always that limitation. Sometimes you win. The book you are writing comes alive. The woman you love wants you.

After all, Bruce did not know. He knew nothing. Anyway he had enough of the wheel-varnishing job and spring was coming. Had he not seen the advertisement he would have quit presently. When he saw it he smiled over the notion of Tom Wills, cursing the newspapers. "Newspapers have some use anyway," he thought.

Since Bruce had been in Old Harbor he had spent very little money and so he had silver to jingle in his pocket. He wanted to apply for the place personally and so he quit on the day before he saw her. A letter would have spoiled everything. If she were what he thought, what he wanted to think her, the writing of a letter would have settled matters at once. She wouldn't have bothered with a reply. What puzzled him most was Sponge Martin, who only smiled knowingly when Bruce announced his intention of quitting. How did the little cuss know? When Sponge found out what he was up to—if he got the place—well, a moment of intense satisfaction for Sponge. "I spotted that all right, knew it before he knew it himself. She got him, didn't she? Well, it's all right. I like her looks myself."

Odd how much a man hated giving another man that kind of satisfaction.

With Aline, Bruce was frank enough, although he could not look directly at her during their first conversation. He wondered whether or not she was looking at him and rather thought she was. There was a way in which he felt like a horse or a slave being bought and he liked the feeling. "I've been working down at your husband's factory but I've quit," he said. "You see spring is coming and I want to try working out of doors. As for my being a gardener, it is, of course, absurd, but I would like trying it if you wouldn't mind helping me. It is a little rash of me to come up here and apply. Spring is coming so fast and I want to work out of doors. As a matter of fact I am quite stupid with my hands and if you take me you will have to tell me everything."

How badly Bruce was playing his game. His note, for a time at least, was to be a laborer. The words he had been saying did not sound like words that would come from the lips of any laborer he had known. If you are going to dramatize yourself, play a certain rôle, you should at least play it well. His mind danced about seeking something more crude he might say.

"Don't worry about the wages, ma'am," he said, and had a hard time suppressing a laugh. He kept looking at the ground and smiling. That was better. It was the note. What fun it was going to be, playing the game out with her, if she were willing. It might last a long time, no let-down. There might even be a contest. Who would let down first?

CHAPTER TWENTY-FOUR

HE was happy as he had never been before, absurdly happy. Sometimes in the evening when his day's work was done, as he sat on the bench in the small building back of the house further up the hill where he had been given a cot on which to sleep, he thought he was consciously rather overdoing the thing. On several Sunday mornings he had gone to see Sponge and his wife and they had been very nice. Just a little inward laugh on Sponge's part. He did not like the Greys much. Once, long ago, he had asserted his own manhood over old Grey, had told him where to get off, and now Bruce, his friend—— At night sometimes, when Sponge was in bed beside his wife, he played with the idea of being himself in Bruce's present position. He imagined things had already happened that might not happen at all, tried out his own figure in Bruce's position. It would not work. In such a house as the Greys'—— The truth was that in Bruce's position, as he imagined it, he would have been confused by the house itself, by the furniture of the house, by the grounds about the house. That time he had got Fred Grey's father at a disadvantage he had him in his own shop, on his own dung-hill. It was really Sponge's wife who most enjoyed the thoughts of what was going on. At night while Sponge was having his own thoughts she lay beside him thinking of delicate lingerie, soft colorful bed-hangings. Having Bruce drop in on them on Sunday was like having in the house the hero of a French novel. Or, something by Laura Jean Libbey—books she used to read when she was younger and her eyes were better. Her thoughts did not frighten her as her husband's thoughts did him, and when Bruce came she had an inclination to give him delicate things to eat. She wanted very much to have him remain well, young-looking and handsome, that she might the better use him in her night-thoughts. That he had once worked in the shop beside Sponge seemed to her a desecration of something almost holy. It was like the Prince of Wales doing something of the sort, a kind of joke. Like the pictures you see sometimes in the Sunday papers—the President of the United States pitching hay on a Vermont farm, the Prince of Wales holding a horse for a jockey to mount, the Mayor of New York throwing out the first baseball at the beginning of the baseball season. Great men being common in order to make common men happy. Bruce had at any rate made life happier for Mrs. Sponge Martin, and when he went to see them and had come away walking along the little-used river-road, to climb, by a path through the bushes, the hill to the Grey place, he got it all and was both amused and pleased. He felt like an actor who had been rehearsing a part before friends. They were uncritical, kindly. Easy enough to play the part for them. Could he play it successfully for Aline?

His own thoughts when he sat on the bench in the shed in which he now slept at night were complex.

"I'm in love. That's what it must be. As for her, it perhaps does not matter. She is at least willing to play with the thought of it."

One tried to escape love only when it was not love. Very skillful men—skillful in life—pretend not to believe in it at all. Writers of books who believe in love, who make love the background of their books, are always strangely silly fellows. They make a mess of it trying to write of it. No intelligent person wants such love. It may be good enough for antiquated unmarried women or something for tired stenographers to read on the subway or elevated, going home from the office in the evening. It is the sort of thing that has to be kept within the confines of a cheap book. If you try bringing it into life—bah!

In a book you make the simple statement—"they loved"—and the reader must believe or throw the book away. Easy enough to make statements—"John stood with his back turned and Sylvester crept from behind a tree. He raised his revolver and fired. John tumbled forward, dead." Such things happen, to be sure, but they do not happen to anyone you know. Killing a man with words scrawled on a sheet of paper is a quite different matter than killing him in life.

Words to make people lovers. You say they are. Bruce did not so much want to be loved. He wanted to love. When the flesh comes in, that is something different. In him there was none of the vanity that makes men so ready to believe themselves lovable.

Bruce was quite sure he had not yet begun to think or to feel Aline as flesh. If that came it would be another problem than the one he had now undertaken. He wanted most of all to get outside himself, to center his life upon something outside himself. He had tried physical labor, but had found no work in which he could absorb himself, and also he realized, after he saw Aline, that for him Bernice had not offered enough of the possibilities of loveliness in herself—in her person. She was one who had thrown aside the possibilities of personal loveliness, of womanhood. In truth she was too much like Bruce himself.

And what an absurdity—really! If one could but be a lovely woman, if one could achieve loveliness in one's own person, was it not enough, was it not all one could ask? Bruce, at the moment anyway, thought it was. He thought Aline lovely—so lovely that he hesitated about coming too near. If his own fancy was helping to make her more lovely—in his own sight—was it not an achievement? "Gently. Don't move. Just be," he wanted to whisper to Aline.

Spring was coming on fast in southern Indiana. It was middle April, and in middle April, in the Ohio River Valley—at least many seasons—the spring is well advanced. The winter flood-waters had already receded from most of the flat lands in the river valley about and below Old Harbor, and as Bruce went about his new work in the Greys' garden, directed by Aline, wheeling barrows of dirt, digging in the ground, planting seed, transplanting, he occasionally straightened his body, and standing at attention looked out over the land.

Although the flood-waters, that in winter covered all the lowlands in that country, were just receding, leaving everywhere wide shallow pools—pools the southern Indiana sun would soon drink up—although the receding flood-waters had left everywhere a thin coating of gray river-mud, the gray was now fast receding.

Everywhere the green of growing things crept out over the gray land. As the shallow pools dried, the green advanced. On some of the warm spring days, he could almost see the green creeping forward, and now that he had become a gardener, a digger in the earth, he had occasionally the exciting feeling of being a part of what was going on. He was a painter at work on a vast canvas on which others were also at work. In the ground where he was digging, red, blue and yellow blossoms would presently appear. A little corner of the vast earth's surface belonged to Aline and to himself. There was an unspoken contrast. His own hands, that had always been so awkward and useless, directed now by her mind, might well become less useless. Now and then, as she sat on a bench near him or walked about the garden, he stole shy looks at her hands. They were very dainty and quick. Well, they were not strong, but his own hands were strong enough. Tough, rather thick fingers, broad palms. When he worked in the shop beside Sponge he had watched Sponge's hands. There was a caress in them. There was a caress in Aline's hands when, as occasionally happened, she touched one of the plants Bruce had been handling awkwardly. "You do it like this," the quick deft fingers seemed to be saying to his fingers. "Keep yourself out of it. Let the rest of your person sleep. Center everything now upon the fingers that are being directed by her fingers," Bruce whispered to himself.

Soon now the farmers who owned the flat lands in the river valley far below the hill on which Bruce worked, but who lived also back among the hills, would be going out upon the flat lands with their teams and tractors for the spring plowing. The low hills, lying back from the river, were like hunting-dogs crouched near the river's edge. One of the dogs had crept near and had thrust a tongue into the water. That was the hill upon which Old Harbor stood. On the flat lands down below, Bruce had already seen men walking about. They were like flies walking across a distant windowpane. Dark gray men walking across a vast light grayness, looking, waiting the time of the coming of the spring green, waiting to help the spring green come.

Bruce had seen the same thing when he was a boy and had walked up the Old Harbor hill with his mother, and now he was seeing it with Aline.

They did not speak of it. As yet they spoke of nothing but the work to be done in the garden. When Bruce was a boy and came up the hill with his mother, the older woman had been unable to tell her son what she felt. The son had been unable to tell the mother what he felt.

Often he felt like shouting to the tiny gray figures down below. "Come on! Come on! Start plowing! Plow! Plow!"

He was himself a gray man like the tiny gray men

below. He was a crazy man like the crazy man he had once seen sitting with dried blood on his cheek beside the river. "Keep afloat!" the crazy man had called to a steamboat plowing its way up river.

"Plow! Plow! Begin plowing! Tear up the soil! Turn it over. The soil is growing warm! Begin plowing! Plow and plant!" was what Bruce wanted to shout now.

CHAPTER TWENTY-FIVE

BRUCE had become a part of the life of the Grey household on the hill above the river. Inside himself something was being built. A hundred imaginary conversations with Aline, that were never to take place in fact, went on in his mind. Sometimes when she came into the garden and talked to him of his work, he half waited, as though for her to pick up, where it had been dropped, a fancied talk had with her as he lay on his cot the night before. If Aline should become absorbed in him, as he was in her, a break would be inevitable, and after a break of any kind the whole tone of life in the garden would be changed. Bruce thought he had suddenly got an old wisdom. Sweet moments in life are rare. The poet has his moment of ecstasy and then it must be put aside. He works in a bank or is a professor in a college. Keats singing to the nightingale, Shelley to the skylark or to the moon. Both men going home afterwards to wives. Keats sitting at table with Fanny Brawne—a little fat, growing a little coarse—using words that jarred on the ear-drums. Shelley and that father-in-law of his. Lord help the good, the true and the beautiful! The household arrangements to be discussed. What shall we have for dinner to-night, dear? Little wonder Tom Wills was always swearing at life. "Good morning,

Life. Do you think the day beautiful? Well, you
see I have an attack of indigestion. I should not have
eaten the shrimps. Sea-food hardly ever agrees with
me."

Because moments are hard to come at, because everything fades quickly away, is that any reason for becoming second-rate, cheap, a cynic? Any little smart
newspaper scribbler can turn you out a cynic. Anyone
can show how rotten life is, how silly love is—it's easy.
Take it and laugh. Then take also what comes later
as cheerfully as you can. It might be that Aline felt
nothing that Bruce felt, that what to him was the experience, the high spot perhaps of a lifetime, was to
her but a passing fancy. Boredom perhaps with life,
as the wife of a rather commonplace manufacturer in
an Indiana town. Perhaps physical desire alone—a
new experience in life. Bruce thought it might be to
him what he made it and he was proud and glad of what
he thought of as his own sophistication.

On his cot at night moments of intense sadness. He
could not sleep and arose to creep out into the garden
to sit on a bench. One night it rained and the cold
rain wet him to the skin but he did not mind. Already
the number of years he had lived had passed into the
thirties and he felt himself at a turning-point. To-
day I am young and can be foolish, but to-morrow I
shall become old and wise. If I do not love fully now
I shall never love. Old men do not walk or sit in the
cold rain in a garden, looking at a dark house drenched
by the rain. They take such feelings as I now have
and turn them into poems which they publish to en-

[229]

hance their fame. A man enamored of a woman, his physical being all aroused, is a common enough sight. Spring comes, and men and women walk in city parks or along country roads. They sit together on the grass under a tree. They will do it next spring and in the spring of the year two thousand and ten. They did it in the evening of the day Cæsar crossed the Rubicon. Does it matter? Men who have passed the age of thirty and who have intelligence understand such things. A German scientist can explain perfectly. If there is anything you do not understand in human life consult the works of Dr. Freud.

The rain was cold and the house dark. Did Aline sleep beside the husband she had found in France, the man she had found upset, torn because he had been in battles, made hysterical because he had seen men in the raw, because once in a moment of hysteria he had killed a man? Well, it would not do to have Aline in just that situation. The picture did not fit into the scheme. If I were her accepted lover, if I possessed her, I would have to accept the husband as a necessary fact. Later when I have left here, when this spring has passed, I will accept him, but not now. Bruce went softly through the rain and touched with his fingers the wall of the house in which Aline slept. Something had been decided for him. Both he and Aline were in a hushed silent place midway between events. Yesterday there was nothing. To-morrow or the day after, when the breach came, there would be nothing. Well, there would be something. There would be a thing called knowledge of life. When he had touched the wall of the house with his wet fingers he crept back to his cot and lay down, but after a time arose to light a light. After all, he could not quite escape the desire to put down something of the feelings of the moment, to preserve them.

I am building me a house slowly—a house in which I may live. Day by day the bricks are piled in long rows, making walls. Doors are hung and shingles are cut for the roof. The air is heavy with the perfume of logs, new-cut.

In the morning you may see my house building—in the street, at the corner by the stone church—in a valley beyond your house, where the road dips down and crosses a bridge.

It is morning and the house is almost complete.

It is evening and my house is in ruins. Weeds and vines have grown in the broken walls. The rafters of the house I aspired to build are buried in long grass. They have decayed. Worms live in them. You will find the ruins of my house in a street of your town, on a country road, in a long street hung with smoke-clouds in a city.

This is a day, a week, a month. My house is not built. Would you come into my house? Take this key. Come in.

Bruce wrote words on pieces of paper as he sat on the edge of his cot and as the spring rains swept over the hill on which he lived temporarily near Aline.

My house is in the perfume of the rose that grows in her garden, it sleeps in the eyes of a nigger who works on the docks in New Orleans. It is built on the foundation of a thought I am not man enough to express. I am not subtle enough to build my house. No man is subtle enough to build his house.

It perhaps cannot be built. Bruce got off his cot and went outside again into the rain. There was a dim light now burning in a room upstairs in the Grey house. It might be someone was ill. How absurd! When you are building, why not build? When you are singing a song, sing it. How much better to say to oneself that Aline did not sleep. For me the lie, the golden lie! To-morrow or the day after I shall awake, shall be compelled to awake.

Did Aline know? Did she secretly share in the excitement that was so shaking Bruce, making his fingers fumble as he worked in the garden during the day, making it so difficult for him to raise his eyes and look at her when there was any chance she might be looking at him? "Well, well, take it easy. Don't worry. You haven't done anything yet," he told himself. After all, the whole thing, his applying for the place in the garden, the being near her, was but an adventure, one of the adventures of life, the sort of adventure perhaps he had secretly been seeking when he left Chicago. A series of adventures—little glowing moments, flashes in darkness, and then utter darkness and death. He had been told that some of the bright-colored insects that already on warm days invaded the garden lived but for a day. No good dying, however, before your moment came, killing the moment by too much thinking.

It was a fresh adventure each day when she came into the garden to direct his work. Now there was some use for the gowns she had bought in Paris during the month after Fred had left. If they were unfitted for morning wear in a garden, did it matter? She did not put them on until after Fred left in the morning. There were two servants in the house, but they were both negresses. Negro women have an instinctive understanding. They say nothing, being wise in woman-lore. What they can get they take. That is understood.

Fred left at eight, driving sometimes, sometimes walking away down the hill. He did not speak to Bruce or look at him. There was no doubt he disliked the idea of the young white man working in the garden. His dislike of the idea was in his shoulders, in the lines of his back, as he walked away. It gave Bruce a kind of half-ugly satisfaction. Why? The man, her husband, he had told himself, did not matter, did not exist—at least not in the world of his fancy.

The adventure lay in her coming out of the house, being near him sometimes for an hour or two in the morning and for another hour or two in the afternoon. He shared in her plans for the garden, did things carefully as she directed. She spoke and he heard her voice. When he thought her back was turned, or when, as happened sometimes on warm mornings, she sat on a bench, some distance away, and pretended to read a book, he stole furtive glances. How good that her husband could buy her expensive and simple gowns, well-made shoes. The fact of the big wheel company going on down the river, of Sponge Martin varnishing automobile wheels, began to have a point. He had himself worked in the factory for some months, and had varnished a certain number of wheels. Some pennies of the profits from his own labor had perhaps gone into buying things for her to wear, a bit of lace about the wrists, a quarter-yard of the cloth that made the dress she wore. Good to look at her and smile at one's own thoughts, play with one's own thoughts. One might as well take things as they are. He, himself, could never be a successful manufacturer. As for her being Fred Grey's wife. If a painter has painted a canvas and has hung it, does it remain his canvas? If a man has written a poem, does it remain his poem? What absurdity! As for Fred Grey—he should have been glad. If he loved her, how good to think another loved also. You are doing well, Mr. Grey. Do 'tend up to your affairs. Make money. Buy her many beautiful things. I do not know how to do it. If the shoe were on the other foot. Well, you see, it isn't. It couldn't be. Why think of it?

The situation the better really that Aline did not belong to Bruce, that she belonged to another. If she belonged to him he would have to go into the house with her, sit down with her at table, see too much of her. The worst was that she would see too much of him. She would find out about him. That was hardly the point of his adventure. Now, as matters stood, she could, if the fancy came to her, think of him as he thought of her, and he would do nothing to disturb her thoughts. "Life is better," Bruce whispered to himself, "now that men and women have become civilized enough not to want to see too much of each other. Marriage is a relic of barbarism. It is the civilized man who clothes himself and his women, develops his decorative sense in the process. Once men did not even clothe the bodies of themselves or their women. Stinking hides drying on the floor of a cave. Later they learned to clothe not only the body but all the details of life. Sewerage came into vogue, ladies of the court of the early French kings— the Medici ladies, too—must have smelled abominably before they learned to douse themselves with scents."

Nowdays houses were built that allowed somewhat for separate existence, individual existence within the walls of the house. Better if men built their houses even more judiciously, separated themselves more and more.

Let lovers creep in. Yourself become a lover creeping, creeping. What makes you think you are too ugly to be a lover? What the world wanted was more lovers and fewer husbands and wives. Bruce did not think much concerning the soundness of his thoughts. Would you question the soundness of Cézanne's thoughts as he stood before the canvas? Would you question the soundness of Keats' thoughts as he sang?

Much better that Aline, his lady, belonged to Fred Grey—a manufacturer of the town of Old Harbor in Indiana. Why have factories in towns like Old Harbor if no Alines are to result? Are we to remain always barbarians?

In another mood Bruce might well wonder how much Fred Grey knew, how much he was capable of knowing. Can anything happen in the world without all concerned knowing?

They would try, however, to suppress their own knowledge. How natural and human to do so. In war or in peace we do not kill the man we hate. We try to kill the thing we hate in ourselves.

CHAPTER TWENTY-SIX

FRED GREY walked down the path to the gate in the morning. Sometimes he turned and looked at Bruce. The two men had not as yet spoken to each other.

No man likes the thought of another man, a white man, rather good to look upon, alone all day with his wife in a garden—no one else about but two negro women. Negro women have no moral sense. They will do anything. They like it maybe, don't pretend not to like it. That's what makes the whites so angry about them when they think about it. Such cattle! If we can't have good serious men in this country what are we coming to?

One afternoon in May, Bruce had been down into the town to buy some needed garden-tools, and he was walking back up the hill and there was Fred Grey walking just ahead of him. Fred was younger than himself but was some two or three inches shorter.

Now that he sat all day at a desk in the factory office and lived well, Fred was inclined to grow fat. He had developed a paunch and his cheeks had grown puffy. He thought it would be a good thing, for a time anyway, to walk back and forth to his work. If Old Harbor only had a golf-course. Someone ought to promote one. The trouble was that there were not enough people of his class in town to support a country club.

The two men were climbing up the hill and Fred was aware of Bruce's presence behind him. How unfortunate! If he had been behind, with Bruce in front, he could have regulated his own pace and could have spent the time as he walked along sizing the man up. After having glanced back and seen Bruce he did not turn again. Had Bruce known that he had turned his head to look? It was a question, one of those annoying little questions that can so get on a man's nerves.

When Bruce had come to work in the Greys' garden Fred had at once recognized him as the man who had worked in the factory beside Sponge Martin, and had asked Aline about him, but she had replied by merely shaking her head. "Really, I know nothing about him, but he works very well," she had said. How could you go back of that? You couldn't. To imply, to suggest anything. Impossible! A man can't be a barbarian like that.

If Aline hadn't loved him why had she married him? If he had married a poor girl then he might have grounds for suspicion, but Aline's father was a good sound man and had a big law-practice in Chicago. A lady is a lady. That's one advantage of marrying a lady. You don't have to be always asking yourself questions.

When you are walking up a hill before a man who is your gardener what is the best thing to do? In the time of Fred's grandfather and even in his father's time all men in Indiana small towns were pretty much alike. Anyway they thought they were pretty much alike, but times had changed.

The street up which Fred was climbing was one of the most exclusive in Old Harbor. Doctors and lawyers, a bank cashier, the best people in town lived up there now. Fred had rather got the jump on them because the house at the very top of the hill had belonged to his family for three generations. Three generations in an Indiana town, particularly if you have money, means something.

That gardener Aline had hired was always about with Sponge Martin when he worked down at the factory; and of Sponge, Fred had a memory. When he was a boy, he went down to Sponge's carriage-painting shop with his father and there was a row. A good thing, Fred thought, that times had changed, I'd fire that Sponge, only—— The trouble was that Sponge had lived in the town since he was a boy. Everyone knew him and everyone liked him. You don't want to get a town down on you if you have to live there. And then, too, Sponge was a good workman, no doubt of that. The foreman said he could do more work than any other man in his department and do it with one hand tied behind him. A man had to realize his obligations. Just because you own or control a factory you can't treat men as you please! There is an obligation implied in the control of capital. You've got to realize that.

If Fred waited for Bruce, walked up the hill beside him, past the houses scattered along the hill, what then? What would the two men talk about? "I don't like the looks of him much," Fred told himself. He wondered why.

There was a certain tone a factory-owner like himself simply had to take toward the men who worked for him. When you are in the army it's different, of course.

Had Fred been driving his car that evening it would have been easy enough to stop and offer the gardener a lift. That's something different. It puts things on a different basis. If you are driving a good car you stop and say, "Jump in." It's nice. It's democratic and at the same time you are all right. Well, you see, you own the car, after all. You shift the gears, step on the gas. There is something to talk about. There isn't any question of whether or not one man puffs a bit more than the other, climbing a hill. No one puffs. You speak about the car, growl about it a little. "Yes, it's a good enough car, but the upkeep is too much. Sometimes I think I will sell it and buy a Ford." You praise the Ford, speak of Henry Ford as a great man. "He's the kind of man we ought to have as President. What we need is a good careful business administration." You speak of Henry Ford without any tinge of jealousy, show you are a broad-minded man. "That peace-ship idea he had was kinda nutty, don't you think? Yes, but he has sure wiped that all out since."

But afoot! On your own legs! A man ought to cut out smoking so much. Fred had done too much sitting at a desk since he had got out of the army.

Sometimes he read articles in the magazines or newspapers. Such and such a great business man was careful about his diet. In the evening before going to bed he drank a glass of milk and ate a cracker. In the morning he got up early and took a brisk walk. Head clear for business. Damn! You get a good car and then you walk, to improve your wind, to keep in shape. Aline was right not to care much for driving about in the evening in the car. She liked to work in her garden. Aline had a good figure. Fred was proud of his wife. A fine little woman.

Fred had a story about life in the army he liked to tell sometimes to Harcourt or to some traveling man—"You can't tell how men will turn out when they are put to the test. In the army we had big men and little men. You would think, now wouldn't you, that the big men would stand the grind the best? Well, you would be fooled. We had a fellow in our company, only weighed a hundred and eighteen. At home he had been a drug-clerk or something like that. He hardly ate enough to keep a sparrow alive, always seemed about to die, but he was a fooler. Gee, he was tough. He lasted and lasted."

"Better walk a little faster, avoid an embarrassing situation"—Fred thought. He increased his pace, not too much. He didn't want the fellow behind him to know he was trying to avoid him. The fool might think he was afraid of something.

Thoughts going on. Fred didn't like such thoughts. Why in hell hadn't Aline been satisfied with the negro gardener?

Well, a man couldn't say to his wife—"I don't like the looks of things here. I don't like the idea of a

young white man alone with you all day in the garden."
A man might imply—what—well, physical danger. If
he did she would laugh.

To say too much would imply—— Well, something
like an equality between himself and Bruce. That sort
of thing was all right in the army. You had to do it
there. But in civil life—— To say anything would
be to say too much, to imply too much.

Damn!

Better to walk faster. Show him that although a
man sits all day at a desk, keeping things going for just
such laboring-men as himself, keeping their wages coming in, people's children fed, all that sort of thing, that
in spite of everything a man's legs and wind are all
right.

Fred had got to the Greys' front gate but a few steps
ahead of Bruce, and had immediately gone into the
house without looking back. The walk had been a sort
of revelation to Bruce. This business of building himself up, in his own mind, as a man asking nothing—
nothing but the privilege of loving.

There had been a rather nasty inclination to taunt
her husband, make him feel uncomfortable. The footsteps of the gardener had constantly drawn nearer and
nearer. A sharp click-click, of heavy shoes at first
on a cement sidewalk and then on a brick pavement.
Bruce's wind was good. He did not mind climbing.
Well, he had seen Fred look around. He knew what
was going on in Fred's mind.

Fred—listening to the footsteps—"I wish some of
the men who work for me at the factory would show

that much life. I'll bet when he worked at the factory he never hurried to his job."

Bruce—with a smile on his lips—a rather mean feeling of satisfaction within.

"He is afraid. Then he knows. He knows but is afraid to know."

As they neared the top of the hill Fred had an inclination to run, but checked it. There was an attempt at dignity. The man's back told Bruce what he wanted to know. He remembered the man Smedley who had been such a delight to Sponge.

"We men are pleasant things. There is so much good-will in us."

He had got almost to the place where he could by a special effort step on Fred's heels.

Inside something singing—a challenge. "I could if I wanted to. I could if I wanted to."

Could what?

BOOK NINE

CHAPTER TWENTY-SEVEN

SHE had got him near her and he seemed to her dumb, afraid to speak for himself. How bold one can be in fancy and how very difficult it is to be bold in fact. Having him there, in the garden at work, where she could see him every day, made her realize, as she had never before realized, the maleness of the male, at least of the American male. A Frenchman would have been another problem. She was infinitely relieved that he was not a Frenchman. What strange things males were, really. When she was not in the garden she could, by going upstairs into her own room, sit and look at him. He was trying so earnestly to be a gardener, making such a bungle of it for the most part.

And what thoughts must be going on in his head. If Fred and Bruce but knew how, as she sat by the window upstairs, she sometimes laughed at both of them, they might both be angry and flee the place for good. When Fred left in the morning at eight she ran quickly upstairs to watch him go. He walked down the path to the front gate with an attempt at dignity, as though to say, "I know nothing of what is going on here, in fact I am sure nothing is going on. It is beneath my dignity to suppose there is anything going on. To allow there was anything going on would be too much of a come-down. You see how it is. Watch my back as I walk along. You see, don't you, how unperturbed I am? I'm Fred Grey, am I not? As for these upstarts——!"

All right for a woman to play but she must not play too long. The males have her there.

Aline was no longer young, but her body as yet retained its rather finely-drawn elasticity. Within her body she could still walk in her garden, feeling it—her body—as one might feel a perfectly-made gown. When you get a bit older you adopt men's notions of life, of morality. Loveliness of person is perhaps something like the throat of a singer. You are born with it. You have it or you haven't. If you are a man and your woman is not lovely it is your business to throw about her person the aroma of loveliness. She will be very thankful to you for that. It may be what the imagination is for. That at least, to the mind of the woman, is what the male fancy is for. Of what other use is it —to her?

It is only when you are young that you, being a woman, may be a woman. It is only when you are young that you, being male, can be a poet. Hurry. When you have crossed the line you cannot turn back. Doubts will creep in. You will become moral and stern. Then you must begin thinking of life after death, get for yourself, if you can, a spiritual lover.

Negroes singing—

> An' the Lord said . . .
> Hurry, hurry.

Negroes singing had sometimes a way of getting at the ultimate truth of things. Two negro women sang in the kitchen of the house as Aline sat by the window upstairs watching her husband go down the path, watching the man Bruce digging in the garden. Bruce stopped digging and looked at Fred. He had a certain advantage. He looked at Fred's back. Fred did not dare turn to look at him. There was something Fred had to hang onto. He was gripping something, with his fingers, hanging onto what? Himself, of course.

Everything had become a little tense in the house and in the garden on the hill. How much native cruelty in women! The two negro women in the house sang, did their work, looked and listened. Aline was herself, as yet, quite cool. She had committed herself to nothing.

Sitting by the window upstairs or walking in the garden one did not need to look at the man working there, one did not have to think of another man gone down a hill to a factory.

One could look at trees, plants growing.

There was a simple natural cruel thing called nature. One could think of that, feel a part of that. One plant sprang quickly up, choking another that grew beneath it. A tree having got a better start than another threw its shadow down, choking the sunlight out from a smaller tree. Its roots spread more rapidly through the ground sucking up the life-giving moisture. A tree was a tree. One did not question it. Could a woman be just a woman, for a time? She had to be that to be a woman at all.

Bruce was going about the garden plucking out of the ground the weaker plants. Already he had learned that much of gardening. It did not take one long to learn.

For Aline, a feeling of life surging through her, during the spring days. Now she was herself, the woman given her chance, perhaps the one chance she would have.

"The world is so full of cant, isn't it, dear? Yes, but it is better to seem to subscribe."

A flashing moment for the woman to be the woman, for the poet to be the poet. Once she, Aline, had felt something, one evening in Paris—but another woman, Rose Frank, had got the better of her.

She had tried feebly—being in fancy a Rose Frank, being an Esther Walker.

From her window above, and sometimes as she sat in the garden holding a book, she looked searchingly at Bruce. What nonsense books are!

"Well, my dear, we have to have something to carry us over the dull times. Yes, but so much of life is dull, isn't it, dear?"

When Aline sat in the garden looking at Bruce he did not dare yet raise his eyes to look at her. When he did the test might come.

She felt quite sure.

What she told herself was that he was one who could, at moments, become blind, let go all holds, drop back into nature from which he came, be the man to her woman, for the moment at least.

After that had happened——?

She would wait and see what next, after that had happened. To ask the question in advance would be to become a man, and that she was not ready to do yet.

Aline, smiling. There was a thing Fred could not do but she did not as yet hate him for his inability. That kind of hatred might come later, if nothing happened now, if she let her chance go.

Always from the first Fred had wanted a nice, firm little wall built about him. He wanted to be safe behind the wall, feel safe. A man within the walls of a house, safe, a woman's hand holding his hand, warmly—awaiting him. All others shut out by the walls of the house. Was it any wonder men had been so busy building walls, strengthening the walls, fighting, killing each other, building systems of philosophy, building systems of morality?

"But, my dear, they meet with no competition behind the walls. Do you blame them? It is their one chance, you see. We women do the same thing when we get some man safe. It is all very well having no competition when you are sure of yourself, but how long can a woman remain sure? Do be reasonable, my dear. It is only being reasonable that we can live with men at all."

So few women get lovers, really. Nowadays few men or women believe in love at all. Look at the books they write, the pictures they paint, the music they make. Civilization is perhaps nothing but a process of finding out what you cannot have. What you cannot have you make fun of. You belittle it if you can. You make it unpleasant to others too. Throw mud at it, jeer at it—wanting it, God knows how badly, all the time of course.

There is a thing men do not accept. They—the men are too crude. There is too much childishness in them. They are proud, exacting, sure of themselves and their own little systems.

All about is life but they have put themselves above life.

What they do not dare accept is the fact, the mystery, life itself.

Flesh is flesh, a tree is a tree, grass is grass. The flesh of women is the flesh of trees, of flowers, of grasses.

Bruce in the garden, his fingers touching the young trees, the young plants, was touching with his fingers also Aline's flesh. Her flesh grew warm. There was a whirling, singing thing within.

On many days she did no thinking at all. She walked in the garden, sat on a bench holding a book —waited.

What things books are, painting, sculpture, poems. Men write, carve, paint. It is a way of dodging the issue. They do so like to think no issue exists. Look, look at me. I am the center of life, the creator—when I have ceased to exist, nothing exists.

Well, isn't that true, for me at least?

CHAPTER TWENTY-EIGHT

ALINE walked in her garden, watching Bruce. It might have been more obvious to him that she would not have gone so far, had she not been ready, at the right moment, to go further.

She meant really to try his boldness.

There are moments when boldness is the most important attribute in life.

Days and weeks passed.

The two negro women in the house watched and waited. Often they looked at each other and giggled. The air on the hilltop was filled with laughter—dark laughter.

"Oh, Lord! Oh, Lord! Oh, Lord!" one of them cried to the other. She laughed—a high-pitched negro laugh.

Fred Grey knew, but was afraid to know. The two men would both have been shocked had they known how shrewd and bold Aline—the innocent, quiet-looking one—had become, but they would never know. The two negro women perhaps knew but that did not matter. Negro women know how to be quiet, when whites are concerned.

BOOK TEN

CHAPTER TWENTY-NINE

ALINE lay in her bed. It was late in the afternoon of a day in early June. It had happened, and Bruce had gone, where, Aline did not know. A half-hour before, he had gone down the stairs and out of the house. She had heard him moving along the gravel path.

It was a warm, fragrant day and a gentle breeze blew across the hill and in at a window.

If Bruce were wise now he would simply disappear. Could a man have that much wisdom? Aline smiled at the thought.

Of one thing Aline was quite sure, and when the thought came to her it was like a cool hand passed lightly over hot fevered flesh.

Now she would have a child, a son perhaps. That was the next step—the next event. One cannot be so deeply stirred without something happening, but what would she do when it did happen? Would she go quietly along, letting Fred think it was his child?

Why not? The event would make Fred so proud, so happy. There was no doubt that, since she had married him, Aline had often been rather irritated and bored by Fred, by his childishness, his obtuseness. But now? Well, he had thought the factory mattered, that his own war-record mattered, that the position of

[257]

the Grey family in the community mattered most of all;
and these things had mattered, to him, to Aline too,
in a way, in quite a secondary way she knew now.
But why deny him what he so wanted in life, what he
at least thought he wanted? The Greys of Old
Harbor, Indiana. They had already gone on for three
generations, and that was a long time in America, in
Indiana. First a shrewd horse-trading Grey, a little
coarse, chewing tobacco, liking to bet on horse-races,
a true democrat, hail-fellow-well-met, putting cash
away all the time. Then the banker Grey, still shrewd,
but become cautious—friend to the governor of the
state, a contributor to Republican campaign funds,
once talked of mildly as a candidate for the United
States Senate. He might have got it if he hadn't
happened to be a banker. It isn't very good policy to
put a banker on the ticket in a doubtful year. The
two older Greys, and then Fred—not so bold, not so
shrewd. There was little doubt Fred was, in his
way, the best of the three. He wanted consciousness
of quality, sought consciousness of quality.

A fourth Grey who wasn't a Grey at all. Her Grey.
She might name him Dudley Grey—or Bruce Grey.
Would she be bold enough to do that? It would per-
haps be taking too many chances.

As for Bruce—well, she had selected him—not consciously. Things had happened. She had been so
much bolder than she had planned. Really she had
only intended playing with him, exerting her power
over him. One can grow very tired and bored waiting—waiting in a garden on a hill in Indiana.

As she lay on the bed in her own room in the Grey house, at the top of the hill, Aline could, by turning her head on the pillow, see along the skyline, above the hedge that surrounded the garden, the upper part of the figure of anyone moving along the only street on the hilltop. Mrs. Willmott came out of her house and went along the street. And so she also had stayed at home on that day when all the others on the hilltop had gone down into the town. Mrs. Willmott had hay fever in the summer. In another week or two she would be going away to northern Michigan. Was she now coming to call on Aline, or was she going on down the hillside to some other house for an afternoon's call? If she came to the Grey house Aline had but to lie quietly, pretending she was asleep. If Mrs. Willmott but knew of the events in the Grey house on that afternoon! What joy for her, joy akin to the joy thousands of people get from some story spread across the front page of a newspaper. Aline trembled a little. She had taken such chances, run such risks. There was in her something of the satisfaction men feel after a battle during which they have escaped uninjured. Her thoughts were a little vulgar-human. She wanted to gloat over Mrs. Willmott, who was walking down the hill to call upon a neighbor, but whose husband would later pick her up so that she would not have to climb back to her own house. When you have hay fever you must be careful. If Mrs. Willmott only knew. She knew nothing. There was no reason why anyone should ever know now.

The day had begun by Fred's getting into his soldier's

uniform. The town of Old Harbor, following the example of Paris, London, New York, thousands of smaller towns and cities, was to express its sorrow for the dead of the World War by dedicating a statue in a small park at the river's edge, down near Fred's factory. In Paris, the President of France, members of the Chamber of Deputies, great generals, the Tiger of France himself. Well, the Tiger won't ever have to argue with Prexy Wilson again, will he? He and Lloyd George can rest now, take their ease at home. In spite of the fact that France is the center of Western civilization, a statue will be unveiled that would give an artist the jimjams. In London, the King, the Prince of Wales, the Dolly Sisters—no—no.

In Old Harbor, the Mayor, members of the City Council, the Governor of the State, coming to deliver an address, prominent citizens riding in automobiles.

Fred, the richest man in town walking in the ranks with the common soldiers. He had wanted Aline to be there, but she had just assumed that she would stay at home, and it had been difficult for him to protest. Although many of the men, with whom he would march shoulder to shoulder—privates like himself— were workmen in his factory, Fred felt rather fine about the whole matter. This was something different than walking up a hillside with a gardener, a workman —really a servant. One becomes impersonal. You march and you are a part of something bigger than any man, you are a part of your country, of its power and might. No man can claim equality with you because you have marched with him into battle, because you have marched with him in a parade commemorating battles. There are certain things common to all men—birth and death, for example. You do not claim equality with a man because you and he were both born of women, because, when your time comes, you will both die.

In his uniform Fred had looked absurdly boyish. Really, if you are going to do things like that you should not grow a little round paunch, your cheeks should not grow fat.

Fred had driven up the hill at noon to put on the uniform. There was a band playing downtown somewhere, and the quick march-music, blown that way by the wind, came distinctly up the hill and into the house and garden.

Everyone on the march, the world on the march. Fred had such a brisk, businesslike air. He wanted to say "come on down, Aline," but didn't. When he went down the path to the car the gardener Bruce was not in sight. Really it was nonsense his not having managed to get a commission when he went into the war, but what was done was done. There would be men of much lower station in the town's life who would be wearing swords and tailor-made uniforms.

When Fred had gone Aline had stayed for two or three hours in her room upstairs. The two negro women were also going. Presently they went down along the path to the gate. For them it was a gala occasion. They had put on gayly-colored dresses. There was a tall black woman and an older woman with a rich brown skin and a great broad back. They went down to the gate together, prancing a little, Aline thought. When they got down into the town where the men were marching and the bands were playing they would prance more. Nigger women prancing for nigger men. "Come on, baby!"

"Oh, Lord!"

"Oh, Lord!"

"Were you in the war?" "Yes, sah. Government war, labor battalion, American Army. Dat's me, sweety."

Aline had intended nothing, had made no plans. She sat in her room pretending to read a book. Howells' "The Rise of Silas Lapham."

The pages danced. Down below in the town the band played. Men were marching. There was no war now. The dead cannot arise and march. Only those who survive can march.

"Now! Now!"

Something whispered inside her. Had she really intended? Why, after all, had she wanted the man Bruce near her? Is every woman at bottom, first of all, a wanton? What nonsense!

She put the book aside and got another. Really!

Lying on the bed she held the book in her hand. Lying thus on the bed and looking out through a window she could see only the sky and the top of trees. A bird flew across the sky and lit in one of the branches of a near-by tree. The bird looked directly at her. Was it laughing at her? She had been so wise, had thought herself superior to her husband Fred, to the man Bruce too. As for the man Bruce, what did she know of him?

She got another book and opened it at random.

I will not say "it matters but little," for on the contrary to know the answer were of supreme importance to us. But, in the meantime, and until we shall learn whether it be the flower that endeavors to maintain and perfect the life that nature has placed within it, or whether it be nature that puts forth an effort to maintain and improve the degree of existence the flower has assumed, or finally whether it be chance that ultimately governs chance, a multitude of semblance invite us to believe that something equal to our loftiest thoughts issues at times from a common source.

Thoughts! "Issues at times from a common source." What did the man of the book mean? Of what was he writing? Men writing books! You do or you don't! What is it you want?

"My dear, books do so fill in the times between."

Aline arose and went down into the garden carrying the book in her hand.

Perhaps the man Bruce had gone with the others down into the town. Well, that was hardly likely. He had said nothing about it. Bruce was not one of the sort who go into wars unless forced in. He was what he was, a man wandering about, seeking something. Such men separate themselves too much from common men and then feel lonely. They are always going about searching—waiting—for what?

Bruce was in the garden at work. He had that day put on a new blue uniform, such as workmen wear, and now he stood with a garden-hose in his hand watering the plants. The blue of working-men's uniforms is rather lovely. The rough cloth feels firm and good under the hand. He also looked strangely like a boy, pretending to be a workman. Fred pretending he was a common man, a private in the ranks of life.

A strange world of pretense. Keep it up. Keep it up.

"Keep afloat. Keep afloat."

If you let down for a moment——?

Aline sat on a bench beneath a tree that grew on one of the terraces of the garden and Bruce stood holding the garden-hose on a lower terrace. He did not look at her. She did not look at him. Really!

What did she know of him?

Suppose she were to give him the ultimate challenge? But how do you do that?

How absurd to be pretending that you are reading a book. The band, down in the town, that had been silent for a time, began to play again. How long since Fred had gone? How long since the two negro women had gone? Did the two negro women, as they walked down the path—prancing—did they know that while they were gone—on that day——

Aline's hands were trembling now. She arose from the bench. When she raised her eyes Bruce was looking directly at her. She went a little white.

The challenge was to come from him then? She hadn't known that. The thought made her a little dizzy. Now that the test had come he did not look afraid and she was horribly frightened.

Of him? Well, no. Of herself, perhaps.

She went with trembling legs along the path toward the house and could hear his footsteps on the gravel walk behind. The footsteps sounded firm and sure. That day when Fred had walked up the hill, pursued by the same footsteps—— She had had a sense of that, looking from her window upstairs in the house, and had been ashamed for Fred. Now she was ashamed for herself.

When she had got to the door of the house and had stepped inside, her hand reached out as though to close the door behind herself. If she did that he would not of course persist. He would come to the door, and when it closed he would turn and walk away. She would see no more of him.

Her hand reached twice for the door-knob but could not find it. She turned and walked across the room towards the stairs that led up into her own room.

He had not hesitated at the door. What was to happen now would happen.

There was nothing to be done about it. She was glad of that.

CHAPTER THIRTY

ALINE was lying on her bed upstairs in the Grey house. Her eyes were like the eyes of a sleepy cat. No good thinking now of what had happened. She had wanted to have it happen, had brought it about. It was evident Mrs. Willmott was not coming to call on her. Perhaps she had been asleep. The sky was very clear and blue, but already the tone was deepening. Soon it would be evening, the negro women come home, Fred come home. . . . One would have to face Fred. About the negro women it did not matter. They would think as their natures led them to think, feel as their natures led them to feel. You can't ever tell what a negro woman thinks or feels. They are like children looking at you with their strangely soft innocent eyes. White eyes, white teeth in a brown face—laughter. It is a laughter that does not hurt too much.

Mrs. Willmott gone, out of sight. No more bad thoughts. Peace to the body, to the spirit too.

How very gentle and strong he was! At least she had made no mistake. Would he go away now?

The thought frightened Aline. She did not want to think of it. Better to think of Fred.

Another thought came. In reality she loved her husband, Fred. Women have more than one way of

loving. If he came to her now, perplexed, upset——
More than likely he would come feeling happy. If
Bruce had disappeared from the place for good, that
would make him happy too.

How comfortable the bed felt. What made her so
sure she would have a child now? She pictured her
husband Fred holding the child in his arms and the
thought pleased her. Afterwards she would have
other children. There was no reason why Fred
should be left in the position in which she had placed
him. If she had to lead the rest of her life living
with Fred, bearing children by him, life would not
be bad. She had been a child and now she was a
woman. Things changed in nature. That writer, the
man who wrote the book she was trying to read when
she went into the garden. The thing had not been too
well said. A dry mind, thinking things out dryly.

"A multitude of semblance invite us to believe that
something equal to our loftiest thoughts issues at
times from a common source."

There was a sound below-stairs. The two negro
women had come home from having seen the parade
and the ceremony for the unveiling of the statue. How
good that Fred had not been killed in the war! At any
moment now he might be coming home, he might
come directly upstairs to his room, the next one to her
own, he might come to her.

She did not move and presently she heard his footsteps on the stairs. Memories of Bruce's footsteps,
going away. Fred's footsteps coming, coming to her

perhaps. She did not mind. If he came she would be rather glad.

. . . . .

He did come, pushing the door open rather timidly, and when her eyes invited he came to sit on the edge of the bed.

"Well," he said.

He spoke of the necessity of her preparing for dinner and then of the parade. It had all gone very well. He had not felt self-conscious. Although he did not say so she understood that he had been pleased with his own figure marching along with the working-men, a common man for the day. Nothing had happened to disturb his sense of the figure such a one as himself should cut in the life of his town. Now perhaps, also, he would no longer be disturbed by the presence of Bruce, but that he did not as yet know.

One is a child and then one becomes a woman, a mother, perhaps. That may be one's real function.

Aline, with her eyes, invited Fred, and he leaned over and kissed her. Her lips were warm. A thrill ran through his body. What had happened? What a day it had been for him! If he got Aline, really got her! There was something he had always wanted from her, some recognition of his own manhood.

If he got that—fully, deeply, as he had never quite. . . .

He took her into his arms, held her hard against his body.

Downstairs the negro women were preparing the evening meal. Something had happened downtown during the parade that had amused one of them and she told the other.

A high-pitched negro laugh rang through the house.

BOOK ELEVEN

CHAPTER THIRTY-ONE

L ATE in the evening of an early fall day **Fred** was walking up the Old Harbor hill, having just made a contract for a national advertising campaign on Grey Automobile Wheels in the magazines. In a few weeks now it would begin. American people did read advertising. There wasn't any doubt of it. One time Kipling wrote to the editor of an American magazine. The editor had sent him a copy of the magazine without the advertising. "But I want to see the advertising. It's the most interesting thing in the magazine," Kipling said.

In a few weeks now the name of the Grey Wheel Company spread over the pages of all the national magazines. People out in California, in Iowa, in New York City, up in little New England towns, reading about Grey Wheels. "Grey Wheels are Go-Getters," "Road Samsons," "Road Gulls." What was wanted was just the right catch-line, something to stop the eye of the reader, make him think of Grey Wheels, want Grey Wheels. The advertising men from Chicago hadn't got just the right line yet, but they would do it all right. Advertising men were pretty smart. Some of the advertising writers got fifteen, twenty, even forty or fifty thousand dollars a year. They wrote down advertising catch-lines. I tell you what, this is a country. All Fred had to do was to "pass" on what the advertising men wrote. They made designs, wrote out the advertisements. All he had to do was to sit in his office and look them over. Then his brain decided what was good and what wasn't. Young fellows who were studying art made the designs. Sometimes they got well-known painters, fellows like Tom Burnside over in Paris. When American business men started after a thing they got it.

Nowdays Fred kept his car in a garage down in town. If he wanted to ride home, after an evening at the office, he just phoned and a man came for him.

This, however, was a good night to walk. A man had to keep himself in condition. As he passed up through the business streets of Old Harbor, one of the big men from the Chicago Advertising Agency walking with him. (They had sent down their best men. The Grey Wheel matter was important to them.) As he walked along Fred looked up and down the business streets of his town. Already he had helped more than any other man to make the little river town half a city and now he would do a lot more. Look what happened to Akron after they started making tires there, look what happened to Detroit because of Ford and a few others. As the Chicago man had pointed out, every car that ran had to have four wheels. If Ford can do that, why can't you? All Ford did was to see his opportunity and take it. Wasn't that just the test of a good American—come right down to it?

Fred left the advertising man at his hotel. There

were really four advertising men but the other three were writers. They walked by themselves, behind Fred and their boss. "Of course bigger men, like you and me, have really to give them their ideas. It takes a cool head to know what to do and when to do it and to avoid mistakes. A writer is always a little nutty at bottom," the advertising man said to Fred, laughing.

When they got to the hotel door, Fred, however, stopped and waited for the others. He shook hands all round. If a man at the head of a big enterprise gets chesty, begins to think too well of himself——

Fred walked on up the hill alone. The night was fine and he was in no hurry. When you climbed like that and when your breath began to come with difficulty you stopped and stood for a while, looking back down into the town. Away down there was the factory. Then the Ohio River, flowing on and on. When you got a big thing started it did not stop. There are fortunes in this country that can't be hurt. Suppose a few bad years come and you lose two or three hundred thousand. What of it? You sit tight and wait. Your chance will come. The country is too big and rich for depression to last very long. What happens is that the little fellows get weeded out. The thing to do is to be one of the big fellows, to dominate in your own field. Already many of the things the Chicago man had said to Fred had become a part of his own thinking. In the past he had been Fred Grey, of the Grey Wheel Company, of Old Harbor, Indiana, but now he was to become something national.

How fine that night was! At a street corner where there was a light he looked at his watch. Eleven o'clock. He passed on into a darker space between lights. By looking straight ahead up the hill he could see the blue-black sky sprinkled with brilliant stars. When he turned to look back, and although he could not see it, he had a consciousness of the great river down there, the river on the banks of which he had always lived. It would be something now if he could make the river alive again as it was in his grandfather's time. Barges steaming up to the docks of the Grey Wheel Company. Men shouting, clouds of gray smoke from factory chimneys rolling down the river valley.

Fred felt oddly like a happy bridegroom and a happy bridegroom likes the night.

Nights in the army—Fred, a private marching along a road in France. You get an odd feeling of being little, insignificant, when you are fool enough to go in for being a private in the army. Still there was that day in the spring when he marched through the Old Harbor streets, wearing his private's uniform. How the people had cheered! Too bad Aline hadn't heard it. He had sure made a hit with the town that day. Someone had told him, "If you ever want to be mayor or to go to Congress or to the United States Senate even——"

In France, going along the roads in the darkness—the men being placed for an advance on the enemy—intense nights, awaiting death. A fellow had to admit to himself that it would have made some difference to the town of Old Harbor if he had been killed in one of the battles he had been in.

Other nights, after an advance—the horrible job done at last. A lot of fools who never were in a battle were always prancing to get in. A shame they weren't given a chance to see what it was like—the fools.

The nights after battles, intense nights, too. You lay down on the ground maybe, trying to relax, every nerve jumping. Lord, if a man only had a lot of real booze now! What about, say, two quarts of good old Kentucky Bourbon Whisky. They don't make anything better than Bourbon, do you think? A fellow can drink a lot of it and it won't hurt him afterwards. You ought to see some of the old fellows in our town. Been drinking the stuff since they were boys and some of them live to be almost a hundred.

After a battle, and in spite of the throbbing nerves and the weariness, intense joy. I'm alive! I'm alive! Others are dead now or torn to pieces and lying back somewhere in a hospital waiting to die, but I'm alive.

Fred walking up the Old Harbor hill thinking. He walked a block or two and then stopped and stood by a tree and looked back at the town. There were a good many vacant lots still on the hillside. Once he stood for a long time by a fence built around a vacant lot. In the houses along the climbing streets nearly all the people had gone to bed.

In France, after a battle, the men used to stand looking at each other. "My buddy got his. I got to find me a new buddy now."

"Hello, and so you're still alive?"

One thought mostly of oneself. "My arms are still here, my hands, my eyes, my legs. My body is still whole. I'd like to be with a woman now." Sitting on the ground was good. It was good to feel the ground, under the nether cheeks.

Fred remembered a night of stars, sitting by a roadside in France with another man he had never seen before. The man was evidently a Jew, a large man with curly hair and a big nose. How Fred knew the man was a Jew he couldn't have said. You can almost always tell. Odd notion, eh, a Jew going to war and fighting for his country? I guess they made him go. What would have happened had he protested? "But I'm a Jew. I haven't any country." Doesn't the Bible say the Jew is to be the man without a country, something of that sort? Swell chance! When Fred was a boy in Old Harbor there was but one family of Jews. The man owned a cheap little store down by the river and the sons used to go to the public school. Once Fred joined several other boys who were ragging one of the Jewish boys. They followed him along a street shouting, "Christ-killer! Christ-killer!"

Odd how a fellow felt after a battle. Fred had been seated by a roadside in France saying over and over to himself the malicious words, "Christ-killer, Christ-killer." Not saying them aloud, because they would hurt the strange man sitting beside him. Rather fun to fancy hurting a man like that, any man, thinking thoughts that burn and sting like bullets, without saying them aloud.

[278]

The Jew, a quiet sensitive-looking man, sat beside a road in France with Fred after a battle in which a great many men had been killed. The dead men did not matter. What mattered was that you were alive. It was just such another night as the one on which he walked up the hill in Old Harbor. The young stranger in France looked at him and smiled, a hurt smile. He put up a hand toward the blue-black sky sprinkled with stars. "I'd like to reach up and get a handful. I'd like to eat 'em, they look so good," he had said. When he said it an intense passion drifted across his face. His fingers were gripped. It was as though he wanted to tear the stars out of the sky, to eat them, or throw them away in disgust.

CHAPTER THIRTY-TWO

ALREADY Fred thought of himself as the father of children. He went along thinking. Since he had got out of the war he had done well. If the advertising plans did not all work out it would not break him. A fellow had to take chances. Aline was to have a child and now that she had started in that direction she might have several. You don't want to raise one child alone. He—or she—ought to have someone to play with. Each child ought to have his own start in life. They might not all be money-makers. You can't tell whether or not a child will be gifted.

There was the house on the hill, toward which he was going slowly up-hill. He imagined the garden about the house filled with the laughter of children, little white-clad figures running among the flower-beds—swings hung from the lower branches of the larger trees. He would build a children's playhouse at the back of the garden.

No need now to think, as a fellow was going home, what he was to say to his wife when he got there. Since Aline had been expecting her child, how she had changed!

She had, in fact, been a changed woman ever since that afternoon in the summer when Fred marched in the parade. He had come home on that afternoon and had found her just awakened from sleep, and what a real awakening! Women are very strange. No man ever finds out much about them. A woman may be one thing in the morning and then in the afternoon she may lie down to take a nap and awaken something quite different, something infinitely better, finer and sweeter—or something worse. That's what makes marriage such an uncertain, really such a risky thing.

On that evening in the summer after Fred was in the parade he and Aline did not come downstairs to dinner until nearly eight o'clock and the dinner had to be prepared a second time, but what did they care? If Aline had seen the parade and the part Fred took in it her new attitude might have been more understandable.

He had told her all about it, but that wasn't until after he felt the change in her. How tender she was! Again she was as she had been that night in Paris when he asked her to marry him. Then, to be sure, he had just got out of the war and had been upset by hearing a woman talk, the horrors of the war had come back on him with a rush and had temporarily unmanned him, but later, on that other evening, nothing like that had happened at all. His part in the parade had been very successful. He had expected to feel a little self-conscious, out of place, marching as a private with a lot of laboring-men and clerks from stores, but everyone had treated him as though he were a general leading the parade. It was only when he came along that the cheers really broke forth. The richest man in town

marching afoot, as a common private. He had sure
made himself strong in the town.

And then he had come home and Aline was as he
had never seen her since their marriage. Such
tenderness! It was as though he had been ill or hurt
or something of that sort.

Talk, a stream of talk from his lips. It was as
though he, Fred Grey, had at last, after long waiting,
got himself a wife. She was so tender and thoughtful,
like a mother.

And then—two months later—when she told him she
was to have a child.

When he and Aline were first married, that afternoon in the hotel room in Paris, when he was packing
to hurry home and someone went out of the room
and left them alone together. Later in Old Harbor,
in the evenings when he came home from the factory.
She did not want to go out to the neighbors or for a
ride in the car, and what was to be done? In the
evening after dinner he looked at her and she looked
at him. What was to be said? There was nothing
to talk about. Often the minutes passed with infinite
slowness. In desperation he read a newspaper and she
went out to walk about in the garden in the darkness.
Almost every evening he went to sleep in his chair.
How could they talk? There wasn't anything special
to be said.

But now!

Now Fred could go home and tell Aline everything.
He told her about his plans for advertising, took
advertisements home to show her, told her of little

things that happened during the day. "We got three big orders from Detroit. We have got a new press down in the shop. It's half as big as a house. Let me tell you about how it works. Have you a pencil? I'll make a drawing for you." Often when Fred went up the hill now he thought of nothing but things to tell her. He even told her stories picked up from salesmen— if they weren't too raw. When they were too raw he changed them. It was fun being alive and having such a woman for a wife.

She listened, smiled, seemed never to weary of his talk. There was something in the very air of the house nowadays. Well, it was tenderness. Often she came and put her arms about him.

Fred walked up the hill thinking. Flashes of happiness came, followed by occasional little flashes of anger. It was queer about the feeling of anger. It always concerned the man who had been first an employee in his factory and then the Greys' gardener, and who had suddenly disappeared. Why did the fellow keep coming back into his mind? He had disappeared at just the time when the change had come to Aline, had walked off without giving notice, without even waiting to get his wages. Such fellows were like that, fly-by-nights, unreliable, no good. A negro, an old man, worked in the garden now. That was better. Everything was better now at the Grey house.

It was walking up the hill that had made Fred think of that fellow. He could not help remembering another evening when he had walked up the hill with Bruce at his heels. Naturally a man who works out of doors, does common labor, has better wind than a man who works indoors.

I'd like to know though, what would happen if there weren't other kinds of men too? Fred remembered, with satisfaction, what the Chicago advertising man had said. The men who wrote advertisements, who wrote for newspapers, all that sort of fellows were really working-men, of a sort, and when it came right down to the scratch, could they be depended on? They could not. They hadn't judgment, that was the reason. No ship would ever get anywhere without a pilot. It would just flounder and drift around and after a while sink. Society was made like that. Certain men had always to keep their hands on the wheel, and Fred was one of that sort. From the beginning he had been intended to be that sort.

CHAPTER THIRTY-THREE

FRED did not want to think of Bruce. To do so always made him a little uncomfortable. Why? There are people like that, who get into the mind and won't get out. They work their way in where they aren't wanted. You are going along, attending to your own affairs, and there they are. Sometimes you meet a man who crosses you in some way and then disappears. You have made up your mind to forget him, but you don't.

Fred was in his office down at the factory, dictating letters perhaps, or he was taking a turn through the shop. Suddenly everything stopped. You know how it is. On certain days everything is like that. Everything in nature seems to stop and stand still. On such days men speak with subdued voices, go more quietly about their affairs. All reality seems to drop away, and there is something, a kind of mystic connection with a world outside the real world in which you move. On such days the figures of half-forgotten people troop back. There are men you want more than anything else in the world to forget and you can't forget.

Fred was in his office down at the factory, and someone came to the door. There was a knock on the door. He jumped. Why was he always thinking, when something of that sort happened, that it was Bruce come back? What had he to do with the man or the man with him? Had there been a challenge issued and as yet unmet? The devil! When you begin thinking such thoughts there is no telling where you will end. Better let all such thoughts alone.

Bruce went away, disappeared, on the very day when the change came in Aline. That was the day when Fred was in the parade and when the two servants went down to see the parade. All afternoon Aline and Bruce had been alone together on the hill. Later when Fred got home the man was gone and after that Fred never saw him again. He had asked Aline about it several times but she had seemed annoyed, hadn't wanted to talk of the matter. "I don't know where he is," she had said. That was all. If a man were to let himself go he might think. After all, Aline had met Fred through the fact of his having been a soldier. It was odd she hadn't wanted to see the parade. If a man let his fancy go he might think.

Fred had begun to get angry, walking up the hill in the darkness. Down at the shop, he was always, nowdays, seeing the old workman, Sponge Martin, and whenever he saw him he thought of Bruce. "I'd like to fire the old scoundrel," he thought. Once the man had been downright impudent to Fred's father. Why did Fred keep him around? Well, he's a good workman. For a man to think that, just because he owns a factory, he is master, is foolishness. Fred tried to say over to himself certain things, certain little pat phrases he was always repeating aloud in the presence of other men, phrases about the obligations of wealth. Suppose he faced the real truth, that he did not dare dismiss the old workman, Sponge Martin, that he had not dared dismiss Bruce when he worked on the hill in the garden, that he did not dare inquire too closely into the fact of Bruce's sudden disappearance.

What Fred did was to fight down within himself all doubts, all questions. If a man started on that road where would he end? He might end by beginning to doubt the parentage of his own unborn child.

The thought was maddening. "What's the matter with me?" Fred asked himself sharply. He had got almost to the top of the hill. Aline was there, asleep now, no doubt. He tried to think of the plans for advertising Grey wheels in the magazines. Everything was coming Fred's way. His wife loved him, the factory was successful, he was a big man in his town. Now there was something to work for. Aline would have a son and another and another. He threw back his shoulders, and, as he walked slowly and had not got out of breath, he walked for some distance with head erect and shoulders thrown back, as a soldier walks.

Fred had got almost to the top of the hill when he stopped again. A large tree grew near the hilltop and he stood leaning against it. What a night!

Joy, gladness in life, in the possibilities of life, all mixed up in the mind with strange fears. It was like being in the war again, something like the nights before a battle. Hopes and fears fighting within. I don't believe it's going to happen. I won't believe it's going to happen.

If Fred ever got the chance to wipe things out for good. The war to end war, to get peace at last.

CHAPTER THIRTY-FOUR

FRED went across a little stretch of dirt road at the top of the hill and reached his own gate. His footsteps made no sound in the dust of the road. Inside the Grey garden Bruce Dudley and Aline sat talking. Bruce Dudley had come back to the Greys' house at eight that evening, expecting that Fred would be there. He had become somewhat desperate. Was Aline his woman or did she belong to Fred? He would see Aline, find out if he could. He would go boldly back to the house, march up to the door—himself not a servant now. In any event, he would see Aline again. There would be a moment of looking into each other's eyes. If it had been with her as with him, during the weeks since he had seen her, then the fat would be in the fire, something would be decided. After all, men are men and women are women—a life is a life. Is a whole life to be spent hungering because someone will be hurt? And there was Aline. Perhaps she had only wanted Bruce for the moment, a matter of the flesh only, a woman bored with life reaching out for a little momentary excitement, and then, perhaps, it might be that she felt as he did. Flesh of your flesh, bone of your bone. Our thoughts running together in the silence of nights. Something like that. Bruce had wandered for weeks, having thoughts—taking a job now and then, thinking, thinking, thinking— of Aline. Disturbing thoughts came. "I have no money. She would have to live with me as Sponge's old woman lives with Sponge." He remembered something that had existed between Sponge and his old woman, an old salty knowledge of each other. A man and woman on a sawdust pile under a summer moon. Fish-lines out. The soft night, the river flowing silently in the darkness, youth past, old age coming, two unmoral, unchristian people, lying on a sawdust pile and enjoying the moment, enjoying each other, being part of the night, of the sky sprinkled with stars, of the earth. Many men and women lie together all their lives, each hungering away from the other. Bruce had done just that with Bernice, and then he had cut out. To stay would have been to betray, day after day, both himself and Bernice. Was Aline doing just that with her husband and did she know? Would she be glad, as he had been glad, for the opportunity to bring it to an end? Would her heart jump with gladness when she saw him again? He had thought he would know when he had come again to the door of her house.

CHAPTER THIRTY-FIVE

AND so Bruce had come that evening and had found Aline shocked, frightened and infinitely glad. She took him into the house, touched his coat-sleeve with her fingers, laughed, cried a little, told him of the child, his child that would be born after a few months. In the kitchen of the house the two negro women looked at each other and laughed. When a negro woman wants to go live with another man she does. Negro men and women "takes up" with each other. Often they stay "took up" all the rest of their lives. White women furnish negro women with endless hours of amusement.

Aline and Bruce went out into the garden. As they stood there in the darkness, saying nothing, the two negro women—it was their evening off—went down the path laughing. What were they laughing about? Aline and Bruce went back into the house. A feverish excitement had hold of them. Aline laughed and cried, "I thought it did not matter enough to you. I thought it was only a momentary thing with you." They talked little. That Aline would go with Bruce was, in some queer silent way, taken for granted. Bruce took a deep breath and then accepted the fact. "Oh, Lord, I'll have to work now. I'll have to be definite." Every thought Bruce had been having had also gone through Aline's head. After Bruce had been with her for a half-hour, Aline went into the house and hurriedly packed two bags, which she brought out of the house and left in the garden. In her mind, in Bruce's mind, there was, all evening, the one figure— Fred. They were but waiting for him—for his coming. What would happen then? They did not discuss the matter. What would happen would happen. They tried to make tentative plans—a life of some kind together. "I would be a fool if I said I did not need money. I need it terribly, but what is to be done? I need you more," Aline said. To her it seemed that at last she also was to become something definite. "I have really just been another Esther, living here with Fred. The test came once for Esther and she did not dare take it. She became what she is," Aline thought. She did not dare think of Fred, of what she had done to him, what she was about to do. She would wait until he came up the hill to the house.

Fred had reached the gate leading into the garden before he heard the voices, a woman's voice, Aline's voice, and then the voice of a man. He had been having such unquiet thoughts as he came up the hill, that already he was a little distraught. All evening, and in spite of the sense of triumph and well-being he had got from his talk with the Chicago advertising men, there had been something threatening him. For him then the night was to be a beginning and an end. A man gets himself placed in life, all is settled, everything is going well, unpleasant things of the past are forgotten, the future is rosy—and then—— What a

man wants is to be let alone. If life would only flow
straight on, like a river.

> I am building me a house, slowly,
> A house in which I may live.

> It is evening and my house is in ruins,
> Weeds and vines have grown in the broken walls.

Fred stepped silently inside his own garden and
stopped by the tree where, on another evening, Aline
had stood silently looking at Bruce. That was the
first time Bruce had come up the hill.

Had Bruce come again? He had. Without being
able, as yet, to see anything in the darkness, Fred knew.
He knew all, everything. Deep down within himself
he had known from the very beginning. An appalling
thought came. Since that day in France when he had
married Aline, he had been waiting for something
terrible to happen to him, and now it was about to
happen. When he had asked Aline to marry him, that
night in Paris, he sat with her behind the cathedral
of Notre Dame. Angels, white, pure women, walking
off the cathedral roof into the sky. They had just
come from that other woman, the hysterical one, the
woman who had cursed herself for her pretense, for her
own cheating in life. And all the time Fred had
wanted women to cheat, had wanted his wife Aline
to cheat, if that were necessary. It isn't what you do
that counts. You do what you can. What counts is
what you seem to do, what others think you do—come
right down to it. "I am trying to be a civilized man.

Help me, woman! We men are what we are, what we must be. White, pure women, walking off a cathedral roof into the sky. Help us to believe in that. We later-day men are not the men of antiquity. We cannot accept Venus. Leave us the Virgin. We must have something or perish."

Since he had married Aline, Fred had been waiting for a certain hour to come, dreading its coming, putting the thoughts of its coming away from him. Now it had come. Suppose at any time during the last year— Aline had asked him a question—"Do you love me?" Suppose he had been compelled to ask Aline that question. What a fearful question! What does it mean? What is love? At bottom Fred was modest. His belief in himself, in his own power to awaken love, was weak and wavering. He was an American man. For him woman meant at once too much and too little. Now he shook with fear. Now all of the vague fears he had kept concealed within himself since that day in Paris, when he had managed to fly away from Paris leaving Aline behind, were to become realities. There was no doubt in his mind as to who was with Aline. The man and the woman were sitting on a bench somewhere near him. He could hear their voices very distinctly. They were waiting for his coming to tell him something, something terrible.

On that other day, when he went down the hill to the parade, and the servants also went. . . . A change had come over Aline after that day and he had been fool enough to think it was because she had begun to love and admire him—her husband. "I have been a fool, a fool." Fred's thoughts were making him ill. On the day when he had gone down to the parade, when the whole town had proclaimed him the chief man of the town, Aline had stayed at home. On that day she had been busy getting what she wanted, what she had always wanted—a lover. For a moment Fred faced everything, the possibility of losing Aline, what it would mean to him. What a disgrace, a Grey of Old Harbor —his wife, running away with a common laborer—men turning to look at him on the street, down at the office—Harcourt—afraid to speak of the matter, afraid not to speak of it.

Women looking at him, too. Women being more bold, expressing sympathy.

Fred stood leaning against a tree. In a moment now something would take control of his body. Would it be anger or fear? How did he know that the horrible things he was now engaged in telling himself were true? Well, he did know. He knew everything. Aline had never loved him, he had been unable to awaken love in her. Why? Hadn't he been bold enough? He would be bold. Perhaps it was not yet too late.

He became furiously angry. What trickery! No doubt the man Bruce he had thought well gone out of his life, had never left Old Harbor at all. On the very day when he was down in the town at the parade, when he was doing his duty as a citizen and a soldier, while they were becoming lovers, a scheme had been concocted. The man would get out of sight, stay out of sight, and then, when Fred was busy with his affairs, when he was down at the factory making money for her, the fellow would come creeping around. All during the weeks when he had been so happy and proud, thinking he had won Aline for himself, she had only changed her demeanor towards him because, in secret, she was meeting this other man, her lover. The very child whose promised coming had so filled him with pride was then not his child. All of the servants in his house were negroes. Such people! A negro had no sense of pride, no morality. "You can't trust a nigger." It might well be that Aline was keeping the man Bruce. Women in Europe did that sort of thing. They married some man, a hard-working, respectable citizen like himself, who wore himself out, became old before his time, making money for his woman, buying her fine clothes, a fine house in which to live, and then? What did she do? She kept another man hidden away, a younger, stronger, handsomer man—a lover.

Had not Fred found Aline in France? Well, she was an American girl. He had found her in France, at a place, in the presence of such people. . . . He remembered vividly the evening in Rose Frank's apartment in Paris, the woman talking—such talk—the tension in the air of the room—the men and women sitting about —the women smoking cigarettes—words from a woman's lips—such words. That other woman—an American also—had been at a place, at a performance of some sort called the "Quat'z Arts Ball." What was that? A place evidently where ugly sensuality had cut loose.

And Fred had thought—Aline——

In one moment Fred felt coldly, furiously angry, and in the next moment he felt so weak that he thought he could not continue to stand upright on his legs.

A sharp hurtful memory came. On another evening, but a few weeks earlier, Fred and Aline had been seated in the garden. The night was very dark and he was happy. He had been talking to Aline of something—telling her, no doubt, of his plans for the factory—and for a long time she sat as though not hearing.

And then she had told him something. "I am going to have a child," she had said, coolly, quietly, like that. Aline could be maddening sometimes.

At such a time, when the woman you have married tells you such a thing—the first child. . . .

The thing is to take her into your arms, hold her tenderly. She should have cried a little, been both afraid and glad. A few tears would have been the most natural thing in the world.

And Aline had told him in such a cool quiet way that for the moment he had been unable to say anything. He just sat staring at her. The garden was dark and her face was but a white oval in the darkness. She was like a stone woman. And then, at that moment, while he was looking at her and while that queer feeling of being unable to speak had hold of him, a man had come into the garden.

Both Aline and Fred had jumped to their feet. For a moment they stood together thus, startled, afraid— of what? Were they both thinking the same thing? Fred now knew they were. They were both thinking

Bruce had come. That was it. Fred stood trembling. Aline stood trembling. Nothing happened. A man from one of the hotels down in the town had gone out for an evening's walk, and having lost his way had wandered into the garden. He stood for a moment with Fred and Aline, talking of the town and of the beauty of the garden and the night. Both had time to recover. When the man had gone the time for saying something tender to Aline had passed. The announcement of the coming birth of a son had passed like a remark about the weather.

Fred thought, trying to fight down his own thoughts. . . . It might be—after all, the thoughts he was now having might be all wrong. It might well be that, on that other evening when he had been afraid, he had been afraid of nothing, of shadows. On a bench near him somewhere in the garden, the man and woman were still talking. A few low words and then a long silence. There was a sense of waiting—for him no doubt, for his coming. In Fred a flood of thoughts, terrors—the lust to kill strangely mingled with the desire to flee, to escape.

He began yielding to temptation. If Aline had her lover come to her thus boldly she was not too afraid of being found out. One had to be very careful. The thing was not to find her out. She had meant to defy him. If he went boldly towards the two people and found what he was so afraid he would find, then all would have to come out at once. He would be compelled to demand an explanation.

He fancied himself demanding an explanation—the

effort to keep his voice steady. It came—from Aline's lips. "I have been waiting only to be sure. The child you thought was to be your child is not your child. On the day you went down into town to parade before others I found my lover. He is here with me now."

If something of the sort happened then what would Fred do? What did a man do under such circumstances? Well, he killed the man. But that settled nothing. You were in a bad mess and only got into a worse. The thing to do was to avoid a scene. It might all be a mistake. Fred was now more afraid of Aline than of Bruce.

He began creeping softly along a gravel path lined with rose-bushes. By bending forward and going very carefully it might be possible to reach the house unseen, unheard. What would he do then?

He would creep upstairs to his own room. Aline had been foolish, perhaps, but she could not be a complete fool. He had money, position, could provide her with everything she wanted—her life was secure—safe. If she had been a little reckless she would soon get over it. When Fred had almost reached the house a plan came into his mind but he did not dare go back along the path. However, when the man who was now with Aline had gone away, he would creep out of the house again and come in noisily. She would think he knew nothing. He would in fact know nothing definite. Being engaged with the man, Aline had forgotten the passage of time. She could never have intended being so bold, being found out.

If she were discovered, if she knew he knew, there

would have to be an explanation, a scandal—the Greys of Old Harbor—Fred Grey's wife—Aline, perhaps, marching off with another man—the man a common man, a mere factory worker, a gardener.

Fred became suddenly very magnanimous. Aline was but a foolish child. To drive her into a corner might ruin her life. In the end his time would come.

And now he was furiously angry at Bruce. "I'll get him!" In the library of the house, in a drawer, there was a loaded revolver. Once, when he was in the army he had shot a man. "I'll wait. My time will come."

Pride now swept through Fred and he stood up straight in the path. He would not creep to the door of his own house like a thief. Standing erect now, he took two or three steps, going, however, toward the house and not toward the place from which came the voices. In spite of his boldness he put his feet down very carefully on the gravel of the path. It would be very comforting, indeed, if he could console himself with the feeling of boldness and yet not be found out.

CHAPTER THIRTY-SIX

IT was, however, of no avail. Fred's foot struck a round stone and he stumbled and was compelled to take a quick step to avoid falling. Aline's voice called. "Fred," she said, and then there was a silence, a very pregnant silence, as Fred stood trembling in the path. The man and woman got up from the bench and came toward him and a sick lost feeling took possession of him. He had been right. The man with Aline was the gardener, Bruce. When they had come to him the three stood for some moments in silence. Was it wrath or fear that had so taken possession of Fred? Bruce had nothing to say. The matter to be settled was between Aline and her husband. If Fred were suddenly to do something violent—shoot, for example— he would, of necessity, then become a direct participant in the scene. He was an actor standing aside while two other actors did their parts. Well, it was fear had hold of Fred. He was terribly afraid, not of the man Bruce, but of the woman Aline.

He had almost reached the house when he had been discovered, but Aline and Bruce, having come toward him along an upper terrace, now stood between him and the house. Fred felt as he had felt as a soldier when about to go into battle.

There was the same feeling of desolation, of being

utterly alone in some strangely empty place. When you are about to go into a battle you suddenly lose all connection with life. You are concerned with death. Death is all about you and the past is a fading shadow. There is no future. You are not loved. You love no one. The sky is over your head, the ground is still under your feet, there are comrades marching beside you, near the road along which you advance with some hundreds of other men—all like yourself, empty machines—like things—trees are growing, but the sky, the ground, the trees have nothing to do with you. Your comrades have nothing to do with you now. You are a disconnected thing floating in space, about to be killed, about to try to escape being killed and to kill others. Fred knew well the feeling he now had; and that he should have it again, after the war had come to an end, after these months of peaceful living with Aline, in his own garden, at the door of his own house, filled him with an old horror. In a battle you are not afraid. Being brave or cowardly has nothing to do with the matter. You are there. Bullets will fly about you. You will be hit or you will escape.

Now Aline did not belong to Fred. She had become the enemy. In a moment she would begin to say words. Words were bullets. They hit you or missed and you escaped. Although for weeks Fred had been fighting against the belief that something had happened between Aline and Bruce, he need make that fight no longer. Now he was to know the truth. Now, as in a battle, he would be hit or he would escape. Well, he had been in battles before. He had been lucky, had escaped whole out of battles. Aline standing there before him, the house dimly seen over her shoulder, the sky overhead, the ground under his feet, none of these things now belonged to him. He remembered something—the young stranger beside the roadway in France, the young Jew who had wanted to pluck the stars out of the sky and eat them. Fred knew what the young man had meant. He had meant that he wanted to be a part of things again, that he wanted things to be a part of himself.

CHAPTER THIRTY-SEVEN

ALINE was talking. The words came slowly, painfully from her lips. He could not see her lips. Her face was a white oval in the darkness. She was like a stone woman standing there before him. She had found she loved another man and he had come for her. When she and Fred were in France she had been but a girl, she had known nothing. She had thought of marriage as just marriage—two people living together. Although she had done a quite unforgivable thing to Fred, nothing of the kind had been intended. Even after she had found her man and after they had been lovers she had thought, she had tried. . . . Well, she had thought she could still go on loving Fred, living with him. It took time for a woman to grow up just as it did for a man. We know so little of ourselves. She had gone along telling herself lies but now the man she loved had come back and she could not go on lying to him or to Fred. To go on living with Fred would be a lie. Not to go with her lover would be a lie.

"The child I am expecting is not your child, Fred."

Fred said nothing. What was to be said? When you are in a battle the bullets hit you or you escape, you live, you are glad of life. There was a heavy silence. Seconds passed slowly, painfully. A battle once begun never seems to come to an end. Fred had thought, he had believed, that when he came home to America, when he had married Aline, the war was over. "The war to end war."

Fred wanted to sink down in the path and put his hands over his face. He wanted to cry. When you are hurt that is what you do. You cry out. He wanted Aline to stop talking, not to say anything more. What dreadful things words could be. "Don't! Stop! Say no more words," he wanted to plead with her.

"I can't help it, Fred. We are going now. We were only waiting to tell you," Aline said.

And now words had come to Fred. How humiliating! He was pleading with her. "It's all wrong. Don't go, Aline! Stay here! Give me time! Give me a chance! Don't go!" Fred's saying words was like firing at the enemy in a battle. You fired hoping someone would be hurt. That was it. The enemy was trying to do something dreadful to you and you tried to do something dreadful to the enemy.

Fred kept saying the same two or three words over and over. It was like firing a rifle in a battle—firing and then firing again. "Don't do it! You can't! Don't do it! You can't!" He felt she was being hurt. That was good. He felt almost cheerful about the notion of Aline hurt. He had hardly noticed the man Bruce, who had stepped a little back, leaving the man and wife facing each other. Aline had put her hand on Fred's arm. His whole body was stiff.

And now the two people, Aline and Bruce, were walking away along the path on which he stood. Aline had put her arms about Fred's neck and she might have kissed him, but he drew a little back, his body rigid, and the man and woman passed him as he stood so. He was letting her go. He had done nothing. It was evident preparations had already been made. The man Bruce was carrying two heavy bags. Did they have a car waiting somewhere? Where were they going? They had reached the gate and were passing out of the garden and into the road when he cried out again. "Don't do it! You can't! Don't do it!" he cried.

BOOK TWELVE

BOOK TWELVE

CHAPTER THIRTY-EIGHT

ALINE and Bruce had gone. For better or worse
a new life had begun for them. Having experi-
mented with life and love they had been caught. Now
for them a new chapter would begin. They would be
compelled to face new problems, a new kind of life.
Having tried life with one woman and failed, Bruce
would have to try again, Aline would have to try
again. What curious experimental hours ahead for
them, Bruce being a laborer perhaps, Aline without
money to spend freely, without luxuries. Was what
they had done worth the price? At any rate they had
done it, they had taken a step from which they could
not draw back.

As always happens with a man and woman, Bruce
was a little afraid—half afraid and half tender—and
Aline's mind took a practical turn. After all, she
was an only child. Her father would be furious for
a time, but in the end he would have to knuckle under.
The child, when it came, would stir the male sentimentality of both Fred and her father. Bernice,
Bruce's wife, might be harder to handle. Still—a
little money. There was no chance her ever getting
him again. There would be a new marriage, after a
time.

She kept touching Bruce's arm, and because of Fred,

back there in the darkness, alone now, she wept softly. Odd that he, wanting her so much and now that he had got her, began almost at once thinking of something else. He had wanted to find the right woman, a woman he could really marry, but that was only half of it. He wanted to find the right kind of work too. Aline's going away from Fred was inevitable, as had been his leaving Bernice. It was her problem but he still had a problem of his own.

When they had gone through the gate, out of the garden and into the road, Fred stood stiff and rigid for a moment and then ran down to watch them go. His body still seemed frozen with fear and horror. Of what? Of everything sweeping down on him at once, without warning. Well, something within had been trying to warn him. "To hell with that!" That Chicago man he had just left at the door of the hotel downtown, his words. "There are certain men who can get into so strong a position they can't be touched. Nothing can happen to them." He had meant money of course. "Nothing can happen. Nothing can happen." The words rang in Fred's ears. How he hated the Chicago man. In a moment now, Aline, who was walking beside her lover along the short stretch of road at the top of the hill, would turn back. Fred and Aline would begin a new life together. It would happen so. It would have to happen so. His mind leaped back to money. If Aline went away with Bruce she would not have any money. Ha!

Bruce and Aline did not go down along one of the two roads into the town, but took a little-used path that led abruptly down the hillside to the river-road below. It was the path Bruce had been in the habit of taking when, on Sundays, he went down to dine with Sponge Martin and his wife. The path was steep and overgrown with weeds and bushes. Bruce went ahead, carrying the two bags, and Aline followed, without looking back. She was crying, but Fred did not know. First her body disappeared, then her shoulders and finally her head. She seemed sinking into the ground, going down into darkness that way. Perhaps she had not dared look back. If she had turned she might have lost courage. Lot's wife—the pillar of salt. Fred wanted to shout at the top of his voice—"Look, Aline! Look!" He said nothing.

The path taken was one used only by laborers and servants who worked in the houses on the hill. It dropped abruptly down to the old road that followed the river and Fred remembered that when he was a boy he used to climb down that way with other boys. Sponge Martin lived down there in the old brick house that had once been a part of the stable of an inn when the road was the only one leading into the little river town.

"It is all a lie. She will come back. She knows that if she is not here in the morning there will be talk. She won't dare. In a moment now she will come back up the hill. I will take her back but in the future life in our house will be somewhat different. I will be boss here. I will tell her what she can do and what she can't do. No more foolishness now."

The two people had completely disappeared. How

very quiet the night! Fred moved heavily toward the house and went inside. He pressed a button and the lower part of the house was lighted. How strange his house seemed, the room in which he stood. There was the large chair in which, in the evening, he habitually sat reading the evening paper while Aline walked outside in the garden. In his youth Fred had played baseball and he had never lost interest in the sport. In the evenings during the summer he always looked to see how the various league teams were getting along. Would the Giants win the pennant again? Quite automatically he picked up the evening paper and then threw it down.

Fred sat in the chair, his head in his hands, but quickly got up. He remembered that, in a drawer in a little room on the ground floor of the house, a room called the library, there was a loaded revolver, and he went and got it, and, standing in the lighted room, held it in his hands. He looked at it dumbly. The minutes passed. The house seemed unbearable to him and he went out again into the garden and sat on the bench where he had been seated with Aline that time when she told him of the expected coming of the child—the child that was not his child.

"One who has been a soldier, a man who is really a man, a man who deserves the respect of his fellow men, does not sit calmly by and let another man go away with his woman."

Fred said the words over to himself as though speaking to a child, telling the child what should be done. Then he went into the house again. Well, he was a man of action, a doer. Now was the time to do something. Now he had begun to grow angry, but did not know definitely whether he was angry at Bruce, Aline or himself. By something like a conscious effort he directed his anger toward Bruce. He was the man. Fred tried to centralize his feelings. His anger would not gather itself together. He was angry at the Chicago advertising man he had been with an hour before, at the servants in his house, at the man Sponge Martin, who had been Bruce Dudley's friend. "I'll not go into that advertising scheme at all," he declared to himself. For a moment he wished that one of the negro servants in his house would come into the room. He would raise the revolver and fire. Someone would be killed. His manhood would have asserted itself. Negroes are such people! "They have no moral sense." For just a moment he was tempted to press the muzzle of the revolver to his own head and fire, and then that temptation passed quickly away.

CHAPTER THIRTY-NINE

GOING softly and silently out of the house and leaving the lights burning Fred went hurriedly along the path to the garden gate and out into the road. Now he had decided to find the man Bruce and kill him. His hand gripped the handle of the revolver and he ran along the road and began to climb hurriedly down the steep path to the lower road. Occasionally he fell. The path was very steep and uncertain. How had Aline and Bruce managed to get down? They might be somewhere below. He would shoot Bruce and then Aline would come back. All would be as it was before Bruce had appeared and brought ruin to himself and Aline. If Fred, when he became owner of the Grey Wheel Plant, had only fired that old scoundrel, Sponge Martin.

He still clung to the notion that at any moment he might come upon Aline making her way painfully up the path. Occasionally he stopped to listen. When he had got down to the lower road, he stood for some minutes. Near him there was a place where the current ran in close to the shore and a part of the old river-road had been eaten away. Someone had tried, by dumping wagon-loads of rubbish, the branches of trees, a few tree-trunks, to stop the river's hungry gnawing at the land. What a silly notion—that a river like the Ohio could be turned aside from its purpose so easily. Someone might, however, be concealed in the pile of brush. Fred went toward it. The river made a soft rushing sound at just that place. Away off somewhere, up or down river, there was the faint sound of a steamer's whistle. It was like someone coughing in a dark house at night.

Fred had determined to kill Bruce. That would be the thing now, wouldn't it? After it was done, no more words need be said. There need be no more terrible words from Aline's lips. "The child I am expecting is not your child." What an idea! "She can't—she can't be such a fool."

He began to run along the river-road toward the town. There was a thought in his mind. It might be that Bruce and Aline had gone to Sponge Martin's house and that he would find them there. There was some kind of conspiracy. The man, Sponge Martin, had always hated the Greys. When Fred was a boy, in Sponge Martin's shop. Well, insults had been hurled at Fred's father. "If you try it I'll beat you up. This is my shop. I won't be hurried into doing bum work by you or anyone else." A man like that, a little work-man in a town where Fred's father was the principal citizen.

Fred kept stumbling as he ran but held the handle of the revolver tightly. When he had got to the Martin house and found it dark he went boldly up and began pounding on the door with the handle of the revolver

Silence. Fred grew furious again, and when he had got into the road fired the revolver, not, however, at the house, but at the silent dark river. What a notion. After the shot all was still. The sound of the shot had aroused no one. The river flowed on in the darkness. He waited. In the distance somewhere there was a shout.

He began walking back along the road and now he had grown weak and tired. He wanted to sleep. Well, Aline had been like a mother to him. When he was discouraged or upset she was someone to talk to. Lately she had been more and more like a mother. Could a mother so desert a child? He again became sure that Aline would come back. When he had got back to the place where the path went up the side of the hill she would be waiting. It might be true she loved the other man but there could be more than one kind of love. Let that go. He wanted peace now. Perhaps she got something from him that Fred could not give, but, after all, she had only gone away for a time. The man was just getting out of the country. He had two bags when he went away. Aline had but gone down the hillside path to bid him good-bye. The lovers' parting, eh? A woman who is married has her duties to perform. All old-fashioned women were like that. Aline was not a new woman. She came from good people. Her father was a man to be respected.

Fred had become almost cheerful again, but when he got to the brush-pile at the foot of the path and found no one there he again gave way to grief. Sitting down on the log in the darkness he let the revolver fall to the ground at his feet and put his face in his hands. He sat for a long time, crying as a child might have cried.

CHAPTER FORTY

THE night continued very dark and silent. Fred had got up the steep hill and into his own house. Going upstairs and into his room he undressed quite automatically, in the darkness. Then he got into bed.

In the bed he lay exhausted. The minutes passed. In the distance he heard footsteps, then voices.

Were they coming back now, Aline and her man, did they want to torture him some more?

If she came back now! She would see who was master in the Grey house.

If she did not come, there would have to be some sort of explanations.

He would say she had gone to Chicago.

"She has gone to Chicago. She has gone to Chicago." He whispered the words aloud.

The voices in the road before the house belonged to the two negro women. They had come up from their evening down in town bringing two negro men with them.

"She has gone to Chicago. She has gone to Chicago."

After all, people would have to stop asking questions after a time. In Old Harbor, Fred Grey was a strong man. He would go right ahead with his advertising plans, get stronger and stronger.

That Bruce! Shoes twenty to thirty dollars a pair. Ha!

Fred wanted to laugh. He tried but couldn't. Those absurd words kept ringing in his ears. "She has gone to Chicago." He could hear himself saying it to Harcourt and others—smiling while he said it.

A brave man. What one does is to smile.

When one gets out of anything there is a sense of relief. In war, in a battle, when one is wounded—a sense of relief. Now Fred would not have to play a part any more, be a man to some woman's woman. That would be up to Bruce.

In war, when you are wounded, a strange feeling of relief. "That's done. Now get well."

"She has gone to Chicago." That Bruce! Shoes twenty to thirty dollars a pair. A workman, a gardener. Ho, ho!

Why couldn't Fred laugh? He kept trying but failed. In the road before the house one of the negro women now laughed. There was a shuffling sound. The older negro woman tried to quiet the younger, blacker woman, but she kept laughing the high shrill laughter of the negress. "I knowed it, I knowed it, all the time I knowed it," she cried, and the high shrill laughter ran through the garden and into the room where Fred sat upright and rigid in bed.

THE END

[319]